I0570444

PLAYING
WITH
MAGIC

The Midnight Witches, Book 1

Carrie L. Wells

WHR Publishing

WHR Publishing, October 2015

Copyright 2015 Carrie L. Wells

All Rights Reserved. This book may not be reproduced, scanned, or distributed in any printed or electronic form without permission from the author, except for brief quotations embodied in reviews. All characters and storylines are fiction and the property of the author.

ISBN-13: 978-0692539101

ISBN-10: 0692539107

Published by WHR Publishing
PO Box 100828
Palm Bay, FL 32910
whrpublishing.com

Cover art by Contagious Reads
Edited by Becky Stephens

For Mum, Andrea, and Gram,
the "witchy" women in my life

CARRIE L. WELLS

PLAYING
WITH
MAGIC

1

BUZZ. BUZZ. BUZZ.

The intercom sounded relentlessly, pulling me away from my video game.

"Yeah, what do you want?" I asked, expecting it to be my roommate. Ashley constantly forgets her dorm keys.

"Oops, sorry, Lizzie," said a disembodied voice with a giggle. "It's just me and Jake."

"Jeez, Ashley. Knock it off. It's midnight."

"Like you were asleep." Her snotty tone did nothing to lighten my mood. And she'd called me Lizzie, again. But, if I was lucky, she'd be downstairs making out for a while longer and I'd have the room to myself until she'd had enough. The last thing I wanted to deal with was my bubble-headed roommate and her newest fling.

As much as I hated it, she was right. I hadn't been sleeping. I was working a new level of *Urban Viking Raid*, a video game I just picked up, and I hate pausing when I'm in the zone. Maybe I'd feel differently if Ashley didn't habitually suck face with her man all over the intercom buttons, but she did. And really, even if it had been the first time, I'd be ticked off. It didn't help that I merely tolerated Ashley, and only for Felix's sake. My best friend had an odd crush on Ashley. It was made even odder by the fact that he's gay. You'd think it'd be tougher for a sorority blonde to win over a gay guy, but she had him snowed with her shiny hair and squeaky, sweet voice. Me? I didn't fall for it. Every ditsy bimbo is a little bit psychopathic if you ask me. Anyone who's taken Psych 101 knows that. And Ashley is one broken nail from killing us all.

"She's all kinds of perky and cute, Liza. How do you not love that?" Felix asked when he realized my room-mate-focused discontent.

Ashley is exactly that, perky and cute. She's only five feet two and her blondeness and bright blue eyes are hypnotic. She wears her traditional West Coast look like a badge in our drafty Boston dorm. She owns tank tops and high, strappy sandals. That's all. It's like she doesn't realize she's not on Venice Beach or Rodeo Drive, or wherever she spent her time in "Cali." I hate when she calls it that. "Cali." Gag. But, I would laugh last. She'd be freezing soon enough. Boston winters don't like the weak nor the southern Californians.

She may be channeling Reese Witherspoon in *Legally Blonde*. Whatever the reason she looks and acts like she does, I don't like her. Besides being perky and cute, she's a prima donna. Ashley's diva qualities—like hogging all the vanity space in the bathroom and offering me the smaller closet—

don't help dissuade me of my opinion.

"You only wear like, what, two outfits? I really need the room for my things. Good fabric needs to breath, you know."

She didn't even give me a chance to comment before she had my favorite T-shirt, an awesome, faded, vintage print of Janis Joplin, thrown on the floor. She continued to discard my clothes and busied herself hanging a flimsy slip.

"So, you need to hang your pajamas?" I asked.

"Pajamas? Are you kidding?" She laughed. Her bell-like voice tinkled in what I took as mockery. "This isn't to sleep in. This is a four hundred-dollar slip dress. Don't you read *Vogue*?"

It's pretty obvious that I don't. My long brunette hair has a wave to it, not the trendy soft curl or straight, shimmery curtain that everyone seems to wear. And most of the time it's pulled back in a sloppy bun, a remnant from my childhood attempts at ballet. My wardrobe, if you can call it that, consists of jeans and T-shirts, a broken in cotton jacket I can wear all year, and a dress that Felix made me buy one day in case I ever go on a date. I won't, but just in case I do, I have a dress that makes me not only uncomfortable but screams that I have breasts.

Felix knows me, and loves me, but he doesn't always understand me. I'm a girl who keeps her boobs under wraps. The last thing I need on a date is to put them out there. It's like false advertising really. The poor guy will expect that they're out all the time and be extremely disappointed when he never sees them again.

Along with my fashion choices, I'm not sure Felix will ever understand my searing disdain for Ashley.

"I've tried to like her. I just can't get past the prissy princess thing she has going on," I'd told Felix about two days after we met my sophomore year roommate. "She's more annoying than Barbie. She's, well, she's Skipper."

"Skipper!" Felix laughed, and I watched his latest energy drink obsession come out his nose like watery blue snot.

"I call 'em as I see 'em. And I saw that on move-in day."

"Well, Skipper is a perfect call. Wait. Isn't there already a Barbie friend named Ashley?"

"No. It's Barbie, Ken, Skipper, and Stacie, who was actually Kelly at first." Embarrassed to know that information, I blushed and turned away. For the record, I remember the oddest things, and most of them aren't worthy of knowing.

"First, how do you know that? Second, and more importantly, does that make me Ken? Oh, I could be Club Ken or maybe Ken has a hot Latino frat brother Juan. I'll be him."

I called him Juan for a solid week until explaining the name to other people became overly annoying.

I settled into my green corduroy beanbag and focused on the game. I closed my eyes, breathed deeply, and hit the play button on my controller. The bright lights and constant motion boosted my adrenaline and I forgot about Ashley.

Placing my noise-canceling headphones over my ears, I turned up my music. I avoid the headphones when I'm alone, but they are a dorm-dwelling necessity. At least now Ashley and buzzer boy would find it tough to compete with the driving bass in my ears. As my *Urban Viking Raid* character, a busty Brunhilde-type, launched into another round of kicking and leaping, I saw her path open. If I could lead her to the right, behind the dumpster, I would be able to climb the fire escape and avoid the sniper fire. I was able to lead her past the sniper and to the roof where she grabbed a ride on a helicopter and soared into the next level of play.

Not ten minutes later, the bass wasn't the only pounding noise I heard. I took off my headphones and looked around confused. Realizing it was someone hammering on my door, I reluctantly paused my game. Felix ran through me as I opened the red door to room 327.

"What the hell are you doing in here?"

He shook out his hand, his knuckles red and puffy. "I swear. I was out there banging on the door for fifteen minutes."

He always starts sounding pretentious when I annoy him. His southern boy charm wanes and he gets all worked up. He's from Florida, but he says it isn't part of the great American South like most New Englanders think. He says it's more like

5

a warm New York than a drawling, Confederate-flag-waving state of *y'all* users.

Maybe he's right. I've never been there. I've never left New England.

Felix looked around the room, his eyes fixating on the television. "Playing again?" he asked, less than impressed with my hobby. Felix loved video games, but he loved socializing more.

"What did you think I'd be doing? I just got the game."

"Any chance I can drag you out? I'm starving. I was coding all day. I need a break."

Felix is a computer science major and a graphic art minor. He's specializing in software development. On a perfect day, he uses his Mac to create amazing video game characters with so much detail that I find it hard to believe they aren't real. On a decent day, he sits and types weird abbreviations and punctuation. On a bad day, he looks through all of the code to find the typos and things that aren't in the right place. I couldn't do it.

I'm a literature major. I don't plan to teach. I don't plan to write a great novel either. I like stories, so it made sense to go into lit. But, ultimately, I want to write story lines for video games. A company would take my characters and plot lines and combine them with someone like Felix's amazing graphics and creative coding. Voilà, a winning video game.

For now I study the stories of the world and write a few

here and there. I do that and enter gaming tournaments. Better still, I win gaming tournaments.

I know it can't be my future profession, but it's a good time. I like getting lost in the games, and if talk can be trusted, video games today are what movies were in the 80s and 90s. Who says art can't be interactive, right?

The thing I don't like about gaming is the male dominance of it all. Female video game characters are all the same. They either have humongous comic book breasts or they're manga-like, doe-eyed, schoolgirl types, also with huge boobs. None of them ever look like me. But I suppose that's part of the fun. It's an escape. I just wish I could escape into characters who are a little less slutty.

Girl gamers aren't typical, and the ones who win are far fewer. Each time I walk into a tournament, the talk starts. Lucky for me, the gaming community is huge. With so many games and platforms and categories, I'm not a celebrity or anything. I get my share of gawks and congratulations, but since I only play locally, I don't have a following or even a reputation outside of Boston. But we have a bigger gaming scene than you'd think. Everyone knows about L.A. and New York, but MIT makes sure we're on the map too. It's a big enough group that even a girl who wins her fair share of cash can go without too much hassle. Granted, maybe that's because I'm the only girl some of these guys have ever seen outside of a game.

They'd never think of talking to me.

No one cyberstalks me for my key insight or looks to follow my social media feeds. Then again, since I hate most social media and couldn't care less what anyone ate for lunch, I don't tweet or insta-anything. If I did, it would be the "real me" and not my gamer self. You don't use your actual name when gaming, after all. I'm no longer Liza Scott when I pick up a controller. I'm *SnarkyGurl27* at that point. No one even knows my real name. Liza? Who's she?

That's fine with me. I don't game for notice. I game because I like it, and I like the money. If you can make some quick cash with a talent, why not? That's my motto at least. Granted, gaming is a cool talent and pays well. It isn't like some athletic ability where I have to sweat. I just play and the money comes. My last three tourneys together grabbed me tuition for a year with room and board. Considering my swanky school, that's a heap of cash.

You wouldn't think a literature major would bother with a fancy college. The economic climate doesn't even ensure that getting a degree in something useful like engineering or accounting will get you a job. But I hadn't planned on Riegert College. I was set for Minute Man Community College, but I won a scholarship. No one I know is dumb enough to turn that down. Besides, I love Boston. It's old and cramped, and it's been under construction since before I was born, but amazing seafood, cool historical buildings, and great people with loud accents populate the place. People may favor New York, or Chicago, or even Miami, but they're fools. Besides, the Red Sox make life interesting. Any team that worships a giant green wall and celebrates its own curse is worth rooting for if you ask me.

I knew I'd be leaving with Felix regardless of what type of fight I put up. Reluctantly, I turned off the console, making sure the game saved my spot, grabbed my wallet and keys, and joined Felix in the hall. He was commenting on my Dr. Martens before I had the door shut.

"Why, Liza? Why?" he pleaded with exasperation.

Feigning ignorance, I smiled at him. "Why, what?"

"Those shoes. Why must you wear those horrible man shoes? This isn't London in the 80s, you know. You aren't a Sex Pistol and you aren't a Ramone. So, why would you wear those?"

"I don't have a new answer for ya," I said flippantly. "I like 'em."

"But with all the fabulous footwear options you have, why those? Do you know what I would give to get away with wearing a pair of Jimmy Choo Samba pumps? And you can afford them."

I can, but only because of the tournament money. I put that away for the sure-to-come rainy day that would follow my graduation. I know I won't find a job paying enough to live on for a few years, so the cash will come in handy.

"I'll buy you some then," I answered. "No reason for both of us to wear shoes you hate."

"Hey now. I like my shoes, but Jimmy Choos they are not. So, where do you want go? The Cock?"

The Hancock Tavern sits right off campus. It's close, but far too friendly and crowded for us most nights. When I want a burger, I don't necessarily want to run into Ashley and her Beta Zeta sisters. Besides, The Cock was loud and the burgers were less than stellar.

"Nah, let's hit Joey's. I could go for a good cannoli. They close at two, right?"

"If we hustle, we can have two. And now that you said it, I need a cannoli."

Suddenly a mass of red hair jutted out past a door frame. "Did I hear 'cannoli'?"

"Hey, Darcy. Wanna come?" I asked. "We're headed to Joey's."

"I'd love to," she said brightly. "Let's go!"

"You're up pretty late tonight, Darce," Felix said, teasing our friend. "Aren't you good Catholic girls in bed by nine on Fridays?"

She smiled, used to his joking tone. While she looked like an Irish dairy maid, all bright copper curls and porcelain skin, her sass mirrored a true Bostonian, as did her reply.

"I'm normally in bed at nine," she said in her sweet, dulcet voice. "I'm just not alone."

Felix laughed audibly. It is pretty funny when the angelic Darcy says something like that. Especially when we know she is only half joking. She and her boyfriend of two years, Dante, a gorgeous Dominican soccer player and upperclassman at Riegert, spent plenty of time together in her dorm room. But, unlike Ashley, Darcy spent plenty of time alone and focused on her art degree too. Last semester she spent the whole term covered in clay, and even now she'd obviously been sketching as black charcoal covered her left hand.

"I'd never be in bed alone if I had a guy like that," Felix admitted. "Keep track of that man. I love soccer players."

"Me too," Darcy added with a smile. "Sorry, Felix. You know he plays for a different team."

I couldn't help but insert my own comment at this point. "Players switch teams all the time, Darce. Maybe he's ready to be traded."

She reached out and punched my arm while Felix snickered and smiled broadly. He and Darcy had the same taste in men, both enjoying the long, lean athleticism of our soccer, crew, and lacrosse teams. And neither of them spends much time alone. It's just that Darcy spends her time with one man, and Felix spends his time with many. Not that he's promiscuous or anything, far from it. He's just a flirt, and it works for him. I'm sure he was out at least three nights this past week, and that would be a slow week.

As we walked to the bakery, fall finally hit the city. The first autumn leaves were turning and a brisk wind picked up. I held my arms open to the breeze, happy to welcome my favorite season after an unseasonably hot few weeks.

Joey's was a great spot for a late night espresso and a pastry. It also had the best cheesecake in town, and I should know. I spent my freshman year—and my freshman fifteen—scouting for the best slice. Other places had a better atmosphere, were a little closer, or offered a better selection, but Joey's had the best taste. Anyone could drown a slice of creamy goodness in berries and syrup. It takes a true genius to make plain cheesecake that keeps its firmness when cut and silkily melts in your mouth. Mario is that genius. Of course, the cannoli rock too.

The brightly lit shop offered a warm place to study and caffeinate, as well as a great place to sober up if you had a bit too much fun. We were there too early in the night for the sobering crowd and too early in the term for the studiers. Instead, a few police officers sat at a table, a carafe of coffee between them, while three bakers worked behind the counter. The man rolling out pie crust waved as we opened the door.

"Hey, guys," he called to us. "It's about time you came in."

"Marco, my man, my buddy, my pal," I called back. "I'm in serious need of a hookup."

"Jeez, Liza. We're here for cannoli, not crack." Felix eyed the cops, wondering if my wording had piqued their interest.

"Whatever. Marco knows what I need." I winked at the older man. He'd owned Joey's since before we were born, the grandson of the original namesake.

Darcy and Felix placed their orders: two cappuccinos, one raspberry cream cannoli, one pistachio covered. I was the odd woman out with my coconut hot chocolate, amaretto ricotta cannoli, and a maple bacon doughnut. I know it sounds disgusting, but it isn't. Without a doubt, those doughnuts are the only reason I passed my chemistry final last year. They're amazing.

Felix grabbed our regular table, a Formica-topped booth in the window. The laminated top is chipped in the front corner and will catch a sweater or jacket if you move too quickly. We sit there every time we go to Joey's. The street light in the parking lot adds a glow to that spot after ten o'clock, almost like a spotlight in the otherwise dim bakery. During the day the overhead fluorescents click and hum, but after dark, they dim them and let the lights in the bakery cases and the kitchen carry most of the burden.

As we sat in our humble booth, we watched out the store window, looking from behind large, red, white, and green letters painted on the glass. The night was clear and brisk with a few leaves and a plastic bag blowing across the small parking lot. The police car was the only thing blocking my vision of the street from where I sat. As I looked at the car, I saw our reflection in the car's windshield. I looked more closely, staring at myself. Something looked weird. It was definitely me, but there was a subtle difference that I couldn't put my finger on in the image peering back at me. There was a blue light surrounding my image, but I figured that was from the streetlight. Then, as I looked harder, the image in the windshield started to ripple, like it was a reflection on the water's surface. I turned away, trying to clear my head.

"You okay?" Darcy asked, cappuccino foam on her lip.

"Yeah, I'm fine. I just thought I saw something."

Felix perked up, leaning toward the window. "It wasn't a rat, was it? I almost stepped on one coming out of Thompson Hall last night. Gross."

"No, not a rat. Just a weird reflection."

Content with the answer, Darcy and Felix discussed their history course. I continued to stare out the window trying to make out whatever I had just seen.

2

AS WE HEADED back to campus, enjoying the fall breeze and what I hoped was the end of our Indian summer, Darcy told us about her wild day at Turn the Page, an eclectic store and coffee bar full of new and used books and trinkets. Starr, the store's owner, liked to keep the store stocked with what she called "uniquities" and they often carried only one of any given item.

"I swear, the place just gets stranger the longer I work there," Darcy explained, pulling her shoulder length curls into a ponytail. "Today, this woman walks in when we open, so that's ten o'clock, sits at a back table, and drinks tea until eight. That's ten hours. She just sat there drinking tea and scribbling in a journal all day."

"That doesn't sound too odd, Darce. I mean, it's a coffee shop," Felix said.

I watched Darcy's face fall with her disappointment in us for not finding this annoyance justified.

"No, it's not," she retorted sharply. "It's a book store that serves coffee. The coffee isn't any good, and you have to go all the way through the store to get to the tables. That takes some determination considering how packed the place is."

I tried to show some empathy for my friend. "Okay, I get it. That does sound weird. At the very least sit outside. It was gorgeous today."

"Right? That's what I thought. I mean the park has better lighting, better atmosphere—"

"And probably better coffee," Felix interrupted, laughing.

When he and I first went to Turn the Page, we thought maybe Darcy brewed horrible coffee. After an entire semester of attempts, hoping each time that we'd get the perfect cup, we realized it had nothing to do with the day, the barista, or the order. All the coffee there was wicked bad. Maybe it had something to do with the machine.

"True. She could have gotten coffee from Hot Dog Vinnie and been happier," Darcy said referencing our favorite vendor. Vinnie had a cart a few blocks south of campus and his hot dogs were worth the trek. They were kosher and actually hot. Luke warm dogs are not my style. I want to see the steam. That, and only Vinnie had cranberry mustard. I know it sounds disgusting, but it's sweet and spicy and tart, and it rocks a hot dog.

"She wasn't drinking coffee," she continued, "so maybe she didn't care. She drank tea all day long. Brought her own tea bags too. She just asked for hot water every forty-five minutes or so."

It did sound a little odd, a woman spending an entire day in a bookstore, not reading a book, buying a book, or drinking the coffee.

"Why sit there then? If you're going to drink your own tea and not buy anything, why even walk in?"

"I don't know. It's like she was waiting."

Felix and I loved Darcy's tales from Turn the Page. It sat in an interesting college neighborhood of cheap apartments, dingy restaurants, and beat-up stores on the south side of Riegert's campus. More often than not there was someone who wasn't a would-be customer asleep on the bench in front the store when Darcy arrived. And she had plenty of stories of odd people coming in asking for even odder items. It got to the point that I'd text her when I knew she had finished a shift and ask for the weirdo of the day. To date, my favorite is still the twenty-something hipster who came in looking for a Shuari shrunken head. Darcy didn't even bother to ask him why. She just pointed him to their "oddities" shelf.

"Waiting?" Felix asked her, primping in a storefront re-flection. We stood at a crosswalk waiting for the light to change and make it supposedly safe to cross the busy Boston street. I looked over at my friend pulling up pieces of his hair and flat-tening others. Then I glanced at my own reflection. Something caught my eye. A silvery blue light flashed next to me in the window. A firefly? A spark of static in the air? Before I could look again, the crosswalk was clear and we made our way to the other corner.

"Yeah. She kept herself busy, but she spent plenty of

time looking out the window and at the front door. Every time someone came in, she glanced at them, and looked them up and down."

"Well, if she were waiting for someone she knew, she wouldn't have to give everyone the once over," I said. "She'd recognize who she was waiting for, right?"

Darcy thought for a second. "Maybe, but what if it was someone she hadn't met yet?"

"Oh, like a blind date. Maybe she was waiting for someone she met online at TeaDrinkerDates.com or some weird site like that." Felix seemed enthralled at the idea. "Who knows, Darcy? Had he shown up, you could have witnessed a true love connection."

"Possibly, but she wasn't dressed for a date. Not a first date at least."

"How do you know?" I asked. I know I wouldn't dress for a date the same way Darcy would. I wouldn't dress to go to the pool the way Darcy dressed to go out with Dante last Valentine's Day. I'd have more clothes on. Granted, she has what my grandmother would call a "lovely figure," but I would feel awkward if I didn't cover up some of it.

"It was like she wore a disguise. She had on huge sunglasses and a scarf."

"Maybe a stakeout then, not a date. She would definitely Isadora-Duncan-up for a stakeout."

18

Darcy and I both asked, "Who?"

Rolling his eyes, Felix asked in mock surprise, "Isadora Duncan? Nothing?"

We shook our heads as his disdain for our lack of any and all things cultural grew.

"She was a famous ex-pat dancer. Lived in Europe. She wore super long, flowy scarves. But she died when one got caught in the wheel of her convertible and broke her neck."

"That's awful," Darcy said. "How do you know these things, Felix? Jeez."

"You'll be happy I do some day when I win us a pitcher of beer at The Cock."

I laughed. He wasn't wrong.

"Glasses and a scarf isn't that weird, you know. I mean she could have been doing anything," I said.

"All day? I mean, she looked like Jackie O. until she took them off."

Felix's curiosity about the mystery woman grew. "What'd she look like then?"

"Gorgeous. And not, 'Oh, she's kinda pretty' pretty. Actually gorgeous. She had the most beautiful dark hair. It was so thick. It just fell out of the scarf and was perfect. She didn't even have to touch it."

"What else?" Felix prodded. "Was she tall, short? Dark, light? A good tipper?"

19

"She was actually. She left me a twenty-dollar bill and it isn't like she had to pay for the water."

"But what did she look like?"

"Kind of normal, I guess. Well, normal for people who come into the store." She paused to focus on the image of the woman in her mind. "She had pretty eyes once she took off the glasses. They were green. Almost sea foam colored. Really light."

Colored contacts, I thought to myself. *No one has eyes that color.*

"I like the sound of this mysterious stranger," Felix decided. "Are you working tomorrow?"

"Saturday? Yep. The late shift. I'll close, so I don't go in 'til two."

"Good. We can all sleep in then."

"Before what?" I asked, suspicious of Felix's plan.

"Before we hit Turn the Page, of course. We can't expect Darcy to figure out this woman all on her own. She'll need our help."

I knew better than to thwart Felix's excited plan making. Even if I protested, I'd end up in tow anyway. That's our relationship. He comes up with crazy adventures and activities; I go along with them. It keeps me from gaming all day, and I can attest to whatever he's done when he tells other people. It's probably super codependent, but we make it work.

"So, we'll head in at about four or so," he explained. "Unless you text us to come sooner. I mean, if she's there or whatever."

By that point on the walk home we were passing The Hancock Tavern. Loud voices and louder music seeped into the street as the bar's doors opened. A pack of girls in matching pink and navy blue T-shirts tumbled out into the night air, tripping over each other and themselves, giggling and singing a Taylor Swift song. I noticed the shiny-haired Ashley among them, and she noticed me.

"Oh, my God! It's Lizzie. Look, girls. It's Lizzie," she screeched as she ran up and uncharacteristically threw her arms around me.

She's little, but she hit me dead on and we both careened to the pavement. She kept talking the entire way down.

"Look, Lizzie, look! It's Beta Zeta." At that, the newest initiates started to sing "You are my sister" to the tune of "You are My Sunshine." Just more embarrassing and ridiculous sorority fun.

"Wow," I said, my voice as lackluster as possible while brushing dirt from my jeans. It didn't convey my annoyance to Ashley, but at least the sober people in the crowd could see I wasn't into the scene unfolding. "Yep, it's me, Li-Za." I stressed the two syllables as I did every time I repeated my name to her.

"Lizzie, I'm so happy you're here." She hiccupped before

21

going on. "I was just talking about you."

"Oh, this should be good," Felix mumbled to Darcy. He probably had the same expectations I did of that conversation.

"Isn't she pretty, girls? I mean, if she did something with her hair and those clothes." She paused and covered her mouth. Regaining composure, she continued. "She could be Beta Zeta pretty even."

I knew I should ignore her, but I draw the line at insults from drunk debutantes. "Uh, thanks for the props, Ash. See you back at the dorm." I moved to walk away, but was stopped.

"No." She lurched at me, clinging to my jacket. "Don't go yet. We'll do a make—" And with that, she quickly and neatly vomited on my shiny, sturdy black boots.

"Those boots need a makeover now," Felix said with a laugh. He moved from the horde of girls surrounding Ashley and over to the bar's side entrance. "Go in and clean up if you can. We'll grab a table and order you a soda."

"I'll need more than soda if I'm supposed to forget this." I waved my arms in a circle trying to encompass the entire situation in one gesture.

As I turned to the door, I saw Ashley empty her stomach once again and heard the gags and squeals of her entourage. Heading inside and straight to the back hallway where the grungy-even-when-clean restroom waited, I saw Darcy scoping out a table while Felix scoped out potential dates.

That's when I ran into Fathom Burke. Full face into his chest ran into him. I don't know how we did it, actually, and there is no chance it would ever happen a second time. I was looking down, fuming as the sickly green liquid ran down the toes of my boots. He must have been looking elsewhere too. Otherwise, one of us would have moved aside and let the other pass.

"Dammit," I stammered backing away and brushing spilled beer off my jacket sleeve.

"Shit, I'm sorry." He tried to wipe off my arm with his hand.

Looking up at the lean obstacle I'd collided with, I changed my tone. "Nah, it's nothing. Don't sweat it. I'm good." I attempted to hurry past him and forget how stupid I must look covered in puke and beer.

"Hey, Liza," the steely green-eyed god said. "We have Social Philosophy together, Doctor Malbrow."

"Oh, yeah, we do." *Did he really recognize me? When did that become a thing?*

"Cool," he said. His voice sounded smooth, like the bottle of the beer he was holding. "So, what are you doing? Want a drink?"

"Well, I'm headed to the bathroom right now," I said before I realized the words were escaping my lips. Even I, a dating novice, knew you should never talk about bodily functions with the hottest guy in the room, or any guy, ever. "Maybe after?" was my attempt at a suave recovery. Kill me now.

"Oh, yeah, sure." *Wait, did he look embarrassed? Why was he embarrassed? I was the idiot who ran into him and then mentioned I had to pee.*

With that, he stepped aside so I could walk past him. It looked like he joined his buddies back at the bar, and I finally made it into the restroom and looked in the mirror.

While my jacket had taken the brunt of the spilled beer, my hair, now dangling down my back, was damp as well. Luckily my boots were made to withstand far worse, and I easily wiped the sticky stomach acid off of them. Catching a glimpse of myself in the mirror, I noticed oddities in my reflection again. This time it seemed discolored. Maybe it was the lights. Bar bathrooms—especially this one, its walls strewn with autographs, notes, and pictures—aren't generally well lit. But the Liza staring back at me seemed disconnected somehow.

I hadn't had a drink, yet I started felt woozy. Suddenly I felt hot and dizzy. My eyes stung as a black ring took over the outer part of my vision. I grabbed for the sink, trying to hold myself up.

It didn't work.

3

"LIZA. LIZA, CAN you hear me?"

My head buzzed as Darcy's voice echoed in my ears. I tried to open my eyes, expecting the bar bathroom's hazy beige light. Instead, Felix, Darcy, a woman in scrubs, and the harsh white light of Boston Regional's ER greeted me.

"Welcome back, Liza. How do you feel?" the woman said briskly but with kindness. She was moving quickly, running a thermometer across my forehead and changing the setting on an IV pump in one fluid motion. "Dizzy? Thirsty?"

"Confused." The woman, a nurse I assumed, flashed a small light in each of my eyes. "What happened?"

"You fainted. Dropped right to the floor," Darcy explained.

Felix made a disgusted face. "And the floor there is nasty. On top of whatever made you faint, you probably have MRSA or swine flu or whatever now." He gagged slightly. He isn't much for dirt, germs, or sick people.

"Fainted? That's crazy. I mean I was looking in the mirror and I got a little dizzy, but—"

"You were dizzy?" the nurse asked. "Any vision changes?"

"Well, yeah, I guess. A little tunnel vision. I don't remem-

25

ber anything else."

She grabbed my chart and scribbled. "Tunnel vision. Okay. Anything else? Fever? Fatigue? Stomach upset? Nausea or vomiting?"

"Uh, no," Felix interrupted laughing. "That was her roommate."

I glared at him. I hadn't forgotten why I'd gone in the bathroom, but I didn't need to relive it. "No, nothing else. Just a little dizzy and dark. I don't remember anything else. I mean, well, what time is it?"

"About two thirty. You were out almost an hour. But you should be fine now. I'll send Doctor Drummond in shortly and bring you back some juice."

"Juice? Why?"

"Well, it can't hurt, and it tastes good," she said with a wink. Then she exited, pulling the cotton curtain closed behind her. I liked her even more now.

My friends and I just looked at each other for a minute. I wasn't sure what to say. Apparently, they didn't know either.

"So, what did they do? To me, I mean. Tests and stuff?" I finally asked Darcy knowing Felix would rather not use words like blood or even bandage.

"They didn't find a bump, a gash, nothing. But they did a CAT scan anyway."

I looked down at the wires running from under my shirt

26

to a monitor and felt others attached with hospital goo to my forehead and temples. Pointing at them, I asked, "And these lovely things are for what?"

"Those are the EKG and EEG leads. Heart and brain monitors. I mean, you were out a long time and we didn't know why. Nothing's come back with any answers though, including the tox screen and CBC."

"The what?" I've watched plenty of *General Hospital* with Nan, my grandmother, but that had far more drama than medicine. I had no idea what Darcy was saying.

"Blood tests. No big deal. They're routine. And they put in the IV. When in doubt, give fluids. It's basically a hospital mantra."

Darcy's mom, Colleen, is an anesthesiologist at a hospital across town. She likes to tell the story of the day she made her move, hoping Darcy would see the glories of medicine. She brought home a stethoscope, some latex gloves, and the game, Operation. However, she soon realized her daughter was made for different things when she used the toys to create a mixed media collage about the current insurance crisis in America. Darcy had been nine. Even then her creative genius was unstoppable. Colleen went out later that day and bought Darcy's weight in art supplies. Everyone should have a mom like that. I wish I did.

Maybe she was like that with some other child. I had no

idea. She took off when I was four years old, leaving me unceremoniously with her mother in South Boston. She cleared out her closet and dresser while Nan and I were at the store buying Hoodsie Cups. We probably bought more, but the ice cream treats are all I can remember. I never ate another one after that day.

Shifting my thoughts back to the moment, I ran my hands through my hair and felt my head. Darcy was right. No bumps. Nothing hurt.

"Do they have any idea why I fell?"

"Nothing has shown up yet. You obviously weren't drinking, although you smell like beer. What's that all about?"

"Oh, I ran into someone. He spilled it on me."

Felix perked up suddenly. "He? A mystery he?"

"No mystery. It was Fathom Burke. I ran right into him, smacked my face on his chest."

"That'd knock me out. Foxy Fathom? He's definitely faint-worthy."

"Especially if you klutzed it up and smacked into him. I'd book it outta there and then faint," Darcy couldn't help but add.

"Hey, I'm in a hospital bed here. Jeez."

"Knock, knock," a voice called from outside the curtain.

"Uh, yeah, come in?" I wasn't sure how to answer that. I could easily see the woman beyond the drape, but if she was going to use the etiquette of a door, so would I.

"Hi," she said, walking over and shaking my left hand after noticing the IV in my right arm. She handed me a cup of orange juice. "I'm Doctor Drummond. How are you feeling, Elizabeth?"

She had bright eyes that seemed to sparkle. They were a clear brown, soft and warm. She had her dark hair pulled back in a sloppy bun, and it looked like she spent most of her time inside, under the hospital's fluorescent lights. She had a light, glowing complexion; her skin a gorgeous, pale porcelain.

"It's Liza. I feel fine. Maybe a little tired, but it's two o'clock, right?"

"I'm sorry, Liza." She pulled out a small flashlight, but unlike the nurse's, this one was hot pink. Motioning toward me, she asked, "Do you mind?"

"Oh, no, do what you need to do."

"Well, I'm sure your friends have mentioned that you were found unconscious on a bathroom floor. This isn't a trend for you, is it? Been feeling dizzy or sick at all?"

"Nope. I've never fainted before. Other than feeling dizzy before I fainted, I've been fine."

Felix decided I hadn't been truthful enough. "She doesn't drink. She plays video games that mess with her eyes, and she doesn't drink anything for hours."

"That's not optimal, I admit," Doctor Drummond commented, turning to the IV pump. "And it could surely lead to

29

this kind of thing. I guess that's the hazard of being a college student."

"That's not the half of it," Felix admitted, spilling all of my secrets. "She's a gamer too. Long hours in front of a television, no food, no water, no sleep. It's her thing."

"Well, if I could make a suggestion," Doctor Drummond said as she turned to me, "maybe it's a bit less of your thing for a few days."

"I'll make sure I eat. How's that?"

"It'd be great if you could rest your eyes a little too."

"Classes just started, so we don't have too much to study for yet," Darcy said. "And we should be able to keep her off the box for a few days."

I disliked being discussed as I sat there, but it was nice to see my friends were concerned.

"All I ask, Liza, is that you drink a glass of water every so often. If you find yourself getting dizzy, grab a bite to eat. That could help. You might want to see an ophthalmologist just to have your eyes checked out. Other than that, you should be all right. If you need anything or if it happens again, give me a call." Doctor Drummond handed me her card. Doctor Julia Drummond, General Surgeon. I don't think many doctors hand out their personal office numbers in the ER and I'm sure fewer surgeons do this, but I was happy to have it.

"Will do, Doctor Drummond. Thank you."

"Well, then I guess that's that. I'll send the nurse right in to disconnect this IV and you'll be on your way."

"Thanks, Doc," Felix said as she left my curtained space. "All fixed up now, Liza. Still smelling like beer, but all fixed up."

The nurse came in and turned off the IV. She looked at the monitor and made a muddled expression. Her face concerned me, but it also caused her to stand still for a second and I was finally able to read her hospital identification tag: *Courtney*. She looked like a Courtney with her warm smile and a smattering of freckles on her nose.

"Liza, have you ever had an abnormal EKG before?"

"No, but I've never had any EKG before."

"Well, I'm sure it isn't anything, but I'll take it to the doctor real quick, just in case." With that she turned to go yet again.

"They'd have noticed earlier if something was wrong," Darcy explained. "It's no big deal. Honestly, those things will read weird if you hiccup."

Courtney returned quickly, proving Darcy right as usual. She removed my IV, took off the sticky pads that held the wires, handed me a stack of papers, and set me free.

We were further from the college than when we started so I sprang for a cab. Luckily, it was a Friday night and there were plenty of them cruising the Boston streets. The ride back was quick and quiet considering there were three of us crammed

31

into the back of a cab that smelled like an Italian sub. That alone should have garnered more comments than we were offering. It had obviously been a long night.

The three of us stumbled from the cab and up the dorm steps. Tempted to buzz my room and disrupt Ashley, I decided against it and made my way to the elevator. Usually, I take the stairs, but I didn't feel up to it tonight.

"Do you want to stay with me?" Darcy asked. "Then you won't have to deal with Pukey von Pukerton."

I laughed. I'd be calling Ashley that from now on, whether she liked it or not.

"Nah, I'm just going to shower and head to bed. Even she won't be able to bother me tonight. I'm exhausted."

The elevator stopped at the second floor for Felix. As he exited, he said over his shoulder, "Good luck. Hope she's alone."

Oh, great. I forgot she had been with Jake earlier. Since he wasn't with her at the bar, I figured she may still be alone. In fact, she may not even be in our room, having chosen to spend the night with her Beta Zetas. If I was lucky, that would be exactly what happened.

I wrestled with my keys, eventually getting the right one into the lock, and walked into the dark room. Unfortunately, the end of my night was going much like the rest of it and Ashley was flopped face down on her bed, her heading hanging off the side. She shifted as I tripped over whatever sat on the floor in the middle of my path. My boot hit something large, but light. I used my cell phone to shine a light on the floor and saw a box addressed to me. The handwriting was a clear, curvy script with a slant to the right. The small letters were formed perfectly and evenly.

I reached down, ready to hoist the box onto my desk. Large enough to fit a microwave, I figured it to be rather heavy. However, if it hadn't been so awkwardly sized, I'd only need one hand to lift it. I tore into the package. I didn't care if I woke up Ms. von Pukerton, although I hoped she would stay asleep. I didn't need to deal with her right now.

Pink Styrofoam peanuts erupted from the box. With no tidy way to dig through the package, I started dumping the foamy pieces on the floor. They covered the dorm's brown-gray industrial carpet, floating around. The static in the air caused them to cling together and pull apart.

I dug, my fingertips barely scraping the bottom flap of cardboard due to the depth of the box. I hit something solid, but light. I pulled it out, wiping away the foam pieces clinging to it.

It looked like a case, something that would hold a disk of some kind. Nothing was written on it, just a plain, black plastic case. Opening it, I found exactly what I anticipated, a disk. But this one had writing: *The Midnight Witches*.

33

Placing the disk into my game console, I picked up my controller. I was exhausted, but I couldn't sleep without knowing what this was. Maybe there was a message on the disk like opening credits to a movie or game, something to explain where it game from and why it was sent to me.

The screen filled with computer-generated fog with Gothic text across the bottom: *Boston — 1648.* As it cleared, I saw a group gathered in a town square. Ominous music played and the shot zoomed in on a woman in the crowd. Dressed entirely in black, she filled the screen, seeming to look out from within the game. I swear she actually saw me.

Shaking off the thought, I watched the perspective shift and zoom out to the crowd again. A large tree stood at the center of the group, a rope thrown over one of its strong branches. A hanging rope, complete with noose.

The game cut to the next scene. The woman from the first scene was running through the woods. A man called out, but wasn't seen. "Margaret. Margaret," he whispered as fog filled the screen again. When it cleared, the game began.

I am a woman in the mob, tracking who I assumed was Margaret through the woods. I chose my path, but there are obstacles along the way. I run into a traveler who offers to give me directions. I come across a woman with a child. They seem to need help, but as I slow to see if I can assist them, she pulls a knife and runs off with a ring and cameo necklace I'm wearing.

I go deeper into the game and come across a small house in a clearing. The moonlight streams in, focusing my attention on a lovely garden. A witch's garden. That's what my grandmother called gardens like this, overrun by medicinal herbs and flowers growing wild. The garden pulls me in and I can almost feel the plants' leaves as my character traces her fingers across them.

I'm drawn to the stone house, choosing to walk down the path to the front door. I reach out, ready to knock on the door, but it opens. The dark-haired woman whose face filled the screen in the opening scene welcomes me with a British accent. "Hello, Elizabeth. I've been expecting you."

Wait! She just called me by name. My actual name. Not SnarkyGurl27. Elizabeth.

It isn't odd for a game system to address a player by handle, but I've never been called by name. And usual it's in text, not voice-over. It takes a lot for a computer voice to sound natural, and the infinite list of names makes it virtually impossible to program the game to recognize them, never mind say them.

The on-screen woman, Margaret, spoke again. "Elizabeth? Are you all right, child? Do come in."

I pressed a button on my controller and my character walks into her house. Looking around, I see her modest

35

furnishings, a wooden plank table, a large hearth, a steaming cauldron, a few chairs, and a braided rug. I wonder where she sleeps until I notice a wooden ladder in the corner. It must lead to a loft.

"Elizabeth, blessed be, dear. Please sit down. I've waited for you."

Me? She waited for me?

"Me? She waited for me?" my character asks the woman.

Whoa! That's not all right. Characters don't speak. Never has my character spoken in a game. And they certainly don't speak my thoughts. Damn, this is freaky!

Once again, my character repeated my thoughts.

"Yes, *she* waited for you," Margaret said, emphasizing the pronoun with a chuckle. "I know this must seem odd; however, there are things you should know before you begin your journey."

"What journey?" the virtual me asks. "Where am I going? In the game?"

"No, not in the game. The game is a guide, Elizabeth, not the journey. You're going forward, of course. Or perhaps it is back." Confused, her forehead creased in thought and I'm overwhelmed by the game's detail. "Forward in my time and backward in yours. I suppose that is the best explanation."

"I'm going back in time? To when? To now? I mean, your now?"

"Not as far back as this, dear. And not until you have met those you need."

"So, not to 1648? That's a relief."

"I assume it is. This is not a good period for our kind after all."

"Our kind?" I ask. "What do you mean?"

"All in good time. Tea?" With that, Margaret moved to the cauldron and ladled out a light liquid, filling two cups.

My character takes the cup. Suddenly my dorm room smells deliciously of mint and flowers.

"Rose mint tea," she said, joining me at the table once again.

"My grandmother used to make this for me." I smile at the memory and notice Margaret's lovely dark eyes and the paleness of her skin. They remind me of someone. I couldn't place her, but she was certainly familiar.

So, now I can smell things in a game and characters remind me of people? This isn't normal. Something's up.

Having heard my thought, Margaret responded thoughtfully. "Normalcy may be something you go without for a while, my dear. I truly thought you'd know more before we met, but I suppose a witch's work is never done."

A witch? What the hell?

Setting down my controller, I got up and inspected the box that initially held the game. I dumped out the rest of the foam pieces, convinced I'd find a note or something else at the bottom. Felix does some great coding, and a prank like this was right up his alley.

I picked up the box, turning it over and over. Nothing. There was nothing there beyond my name and address on the top flap.

I sat back down and focused my attention on the game. Margaret reached for my hand. I felt the warmth from her hand on mine even as I held the controller. I set it down, curious as to whether maybe it was the equipment somehow conveying these sensory experiences. Then I felt the pressure of her hand. Releasing the controller had somehow intensified the occurrence.

Frantic with this new knowledge, I asked, "Who are you? How do you know me?"

"Child, this must be confusing for you. I apologize, but we didn't know how else to guide you through all of this. Without your mother here, you'll need extra direction."

With that, I reached out and turned off the game. Her mention of my mother brought stinging tears to my eyes. That was enough of this for one night.

4

"GOOD MORNING, ANGEL," Felix called from the hallway. "Time to be awake."

"Go away," I grumbled, burying my head under my pillow. The sun coming in the window did not match my disposition at the moment. My mood called for a dark, rainy day for sure.

"I would love to," he said, "but I need waffles, woman. Waffles. Do you hear me?"

I heard him. The whole floor heard him.

"Okay. Give me ten," I called to him, not opening my door.

Stepping out of bed, my feet crushed the bug-like foam pieces scattered across the floor. I had forgotten about the box and the game during my short sleep session. The pink chunks on the floor, however, reminded me quickly.

I tied my hair back before splashing my face with cool water. I don't wear makeup, so there were no mascara rings around my dark eyes. Emerging from our bathroom, I noticed Ashley wasn't as lucky. Her pillow wore a pale outline of her face, complete with blue eyeshadow and pink lipstick.

I threw on some jeans and a fresh T-shirt and pulled on

39

my Dr. Martens again as they were no worse for last night's adventure. I finally opened the door to the hall to a mesh of silly string.

"Looks like you were Zeta-ed last night," Felix pointed out.

My door was covered in crepe paper and balloons in navy and pink, the Beta Zeta colors.

"I'm so tired of getting hung up in the Zeta web every morning. Obnoxious." I tore at the decorations. "I live here too. Jeez."

"Oh, wow, cranky Liza. What a joy!"

"Hey, I didn't come to your room in search of waffles. Give me a minute to warm up."

"Yes, lovey. Of course. You warm up, as long as you do it while heading to breakfast."

"What time is it?" My bearings were off, and while I knew it was morning, the details were hazy. "Eight? Eight thirty?"

"It's almost eleven. I let you sleep, but now I must eat. And I wasn't about to break with tradition because of your ER visit."

Each week since we met, Felix and I hit The Small Stack restaurant for breakfast on Saturdays. Some days it was waffles, as was Felix's mission today, and others it was blueberry muffins, chocolate croissants, or heaps of buttermilk pancakes.

"So, your little prank last night was great. When did you

have time to make such a detailed game?" I slapped Felix's arm, driving home my appreciation of the time and energy he spent on his latest hoax.

He stopped walking and turned to stare at me. "What prank?"

He often denied his stunts until he couldn't deny them anymore, until the moment that it was clearly written that he was the culprit. But he never did it this convincingly. He was many things, but a great liar wasn't one of them.

"Aw, come on, Feel. I give. It was funny, even freaked me out a little. Well played."

"Look, Liza, I wish I had done something after the little ER scare you gave me. But I didn't. Who had time to do anything?"

"So, you didn't have a box delivered to me? You didn't program the game?"

"What game? I'm totally lost here."

"You swear it wasn't you?" I must have looked pretty pathetic because he took my hands then.

"Honey, I don't know what you're talking about. Obviously something happened when you got back to your room. Should we call the doctor you saw last night?"

"No, nothing like that." *At least I don't think so.*

I looked around. We were outside Flanagan Hall now. The sun struck the small reflecting pond in front of the library and beams seemed to shoot back out at all angles. The leaves overhead mixed in shades of green and various yellows working toward orange and brown. A typical New England autumn day. It felt anything but typical though.

"Well, if it wasn't you, then we have some talking to do."

"Great," he said enthusiastically. Felix loves excitement and drama. "But can we get to The Stack first?" Admittedly he loves food even more.

We walked the short distance in relative silence, listening to the conversations of those around us. A few frat guys talked about the drunken Zetas at The Cock last night. We smiled at each other as we recognized Ashley's less than favorable description, "that drunk as hell, short, mouthy blonde chick." Karma works quickly sometimes, and now seemed to be one of them. After all, vomiting on someone's shoes did deserve cosmic retribution.

Since it was past that time when most college students were deciding to eat breakfast, The Short Stack had some seating available. There is nothing worse than standing in line when you're hungry, tired, and hungover. That's the case for plenty of folks who show up between eight thirty and ten thirty in the morning. Our delay gave us a shot at the perfect table.

We walked in, sat ourselves at a corner booth, avoiding counter seats for the first time this semester, and celebrated our success with orders of caramel drizzled drinking chocolate.

"There will be no pedestrian beverages for us today, madam," Felix said to our waitress, Loraine. "We want the good stuff. Your best vintage, if you will."

The older woman, a brown halo of curls circling her head, smiled at my friend. "Drinking chocolate it shall be, sir," she said with a regal air. "Coming right up, guys." She backed away from the table giving a slight bow as she left.

Loraine is a good egg. She reminds me of Vi, the hilarious waitress in Grease, but Loraine is cooler. I've seen her pass a tissue to a crying girl while distracting her date and take the wind out of a drunken guy's sails before he can bother to swing at someone who has ticked him off. She has a way with people, and rumor has it she's a retired Marine. I believed it.

"So, what happened to you last night?" Felix finally felt settled in and ready to talk. "Do tell, do tell."

Sipping my newly delivered treat—it was basically a melted candy bar in cup—I determined how much to tell.

"Well, I found a box in my room. A huge box actually."

"Oh, a present," Felix said, absolutely giddy with anticipation. "What was it?"

"Give me twenty seconds and I'll tell you. Jeez, man." Felix's patience was stretched already. Knowing this I tried to hurry the story along.

"It had a game, a video game. The only thing on the box was my name and dorm room address, and inside it was full of

Styrofoam packing peanuts and the game. That's it. That's why I thought it was you. The game part, ya know."

"A mystery game? Did it have a title? Did you play it?"

"Well, yeah. I put it in and the title came up—*The Midnight Witches*—which sounded pretty cool. The CGI is amazing too. I mean, I could see the single eyelashes on characters as they zoomed in. Whoever it was put a hell of a lot of time into the programming."

Loraine returned again to hand off Felix's pecan waffles and my lingonberry crepes.

"So, what's the premise? How was the story?"

"Well, I didn't get very far. I haven't told you the weirdest part yet, and I mean wicked weird." My Boston accent crept out, making Felix snicker as he stuffed a huge bite into his mouth. I usually sounded normal to most people, but every once in a while when I wasn't paying attention, my accent thickened. If you weren't familiar with the clipped words, you might miss what I was saying.

"Whatever. Let me ask you this. How hard would it be," I began, "to get a game to speak the player's name?"

He pondered the question, giving me time to dive into my plate of breakfast dessert. The thin crepes and warm cream cheese disintegrated on my tongue leaving the tart berries to pop in my mouth. My favorite part. It was like the caviar of the breakfast world.

"You mean the game accessed your handle and a character spoke it?"

"Not exactly."

"Because that wouldn't be too tough. I mean the game already has your handle. I've seen plenty of them refer to the player by name in text form. Maybe one or two that used a well-placed spoken name at the start or end of the game."

"This was different. The character spoke to me directly. And she didn't use my handle. She used my name."

"The game called you Liza? That's tough, but not impossible. I mean, it has access to—"

I interrupted him. "No, not Liza. Not the owner name of my handle. It called me...she called me Elizabeth, and she did it more than once."

"That...well, that's weird. Wicked weird even," he said mimicking me.

"It is, right? Wouldn't it take forever to program something to do that?"

"Yeah, that's intense. I can't imagine how many hours you've have to put in to get a game to access the legal name of a player. I mean, you could. If you got to the player's payment info or whatever. The game could refer to the credit card name maybe."

"It gets even stranger, really. It was like the character was talking to me and the dialogue was meant just for me. The whole thing was surprising."

"Wow. As much as I wish I'd done it, I didn't, Liza. I wish I had the talent."

"I'm telling you, it was crazy."

His mouth full, he didn't wait to swallow before asking, "Are you sure this was about you? I mean, what if the game is set to call everyone Elizabeth? That could be possible, right? I mean, your character could be Elizabeth."

I don't know why I hadn't thought of that, but it was true. If Felix was playing, he may have been called Elizabeth too.

"Crap," I said. "Narcissist much? How self-focused am I?"

"Well, it's a pretty cool coincidence. Don't get too down. It was late, and you had a hell of a night."

"True. Maybe you can play a little today. See what you think?"

"Hell yeah I will. We could use some game time anyway. Granted, it'll have to be after we hit The Page and stalk our mystery tea drinker."

"Ugh," I said audibly. Never one to hide my feelings, Felix was used to my noises of contempt. "I forgot about that. Why are we doing this again?"

"First, because we haven't been to The Page in a while. And secondly, because this woman sounds absolutely worthy of a look. What else do you have going on anyway?"

Actually, I had a paper to work on for my Modern American Short Stories class and statistics homework. Felix wouldn't care, though. He knew I could whip the paper out in as little as an hour if forced to and that I'd do almost anything to avoid looking at the stats assignments. Those excuses would do little to sway him.

"Nothing, I guess. But it's only noon. Darcy won't even be there yet."

"I know." He almost purred as he said it. He was obviously happy about something. "Time to thrift first."

"That is the first worthwhile thing you've said in days." I reached for the bill. It was my Saturday to cover breakfast, so there was no fight from my friend. We set up our alternating schedule last year and we never argued about a check again.

Leaving a nice tip for Loraine, we made our way to the register. Fathom sat at the counter, probably waiting for a take-out order. Felix jabbed me in the side when he noticed my beer-spilling companion from the night before.

Glaring at Felix, I made it clear that neither of us would speak again until we were outside. But Fathom didn't get the message.

"Hey, Liza," he called to me from his seat.

Awkwardly, I looked over to him, nodded, and answered, "Oh, hey."

"Are you all right? I saw you take off in an ambulance last

night."

"Yeah, I'm fine. It's all good. Just got a little dizzy."

"Well, I'm sorry about the beer thing. If you need your jacket cleaned or whatever—."

"Nah, really. I'm cool. I just threw it in the wash. No worries."

"Okay, well, that's good, I guess. But I am sorry." Fathom stood and approached the register, approached me. "Here. Take it just in case you change your mind or whatever," he said, handing me a slip of paper.

I opened my palm and saw seven digits, a cell phone number I guessed.

*Fathom Burke handed me his phone number. And it isn't a dorm extension. It's his number, his direct-right-to-him-no-room*mate-interference *number.*

"Thanks. You're cool. I mean, well, we're cool." I stumbled over my words like an idiot and turned to see Felix smiling behind his hand.

Kill me now!

"Okay. See ya later then." With that, it was my turn at the register.

A few hours later, Felix and I walked into Turn the Page with our thrift store finds, ready to show them to Darcy.

"I can't believe I spent less than twenty bucks," Felix remarked with pride and amazement as he shifted his bags.

"Now I need a cupcake."

We headed to the back of the store, past Starr who was helping a customer. She smiled at us and pointed to a corner in the stacks. I assumed that's where Darcy was hiding and we followed her direction.

"Hey, hey, hey," Felix called out to her. "We have arrived."

"I noticed, as I'm sure did everyone else in the place," Darcy said. She wasn't one for dramatic entrances.

"How goes? Anything exciting?" I asked our friend, taking a stack of books from her hands as she climbed down a small ladder.

"Nothing really." Then she dropped her voice. "But our mystery woman is here," she whispered.

"Really? Where?"

"Exactly where she was yesterday. Don't stare, Felix."

He was already sticking his head around the stacks at the end of the aisle, looking over to the small alcove that held the coffee bar.

"Okay, we'll go over there and order something. Who's working the coffee bar today?"

"Austin is, so don't get anything complicated. He still hasn't figured out much back there."

Austin had worked in the store for almost two years, but he couldn't remember much of anything. He was Starr's only full-time employee, and she let it slip last year at the holiday party that he was also her boyfriend's nephew. His employment status made more sense after that.

"Is a cupcake too complex for the boy genius?" Felix asked.

Darcy laughed. "Nah, he should be able to figure that out. Open box, put on plate, hand over. Well, wait, that is three steps."

"You're both so mean. The poor guy can't be expected to be good at everything." Granted, I was teasing too.

"You mean *anything*. He would forget to come to work if he didn't live upstairs. I heard he came down in his boxer briefs last week. He's a dolt," Darcy added. "Hey, Starr, I'm taking my fifteen."

We walked to a small table by an alcove window. There were two other customers seated at that point, a college-aged guy sipping an iced coffee and flipping through a graphic novel and a woman, complete with headscarf and sunglasses, writing in a leather journal. Our mystery woman had returned.

Felix went to the counter, placed our order, and returned shaking his head.

"I don't know what he'll bring over, but I ordered three chocolates with vanilla butter cream and Italian sodas. I figured he only had to open cans and pour. Maybe we have a chance."

"Doubtful, but a good plan nonetheless," Darcy said, nodding in Austin's direction. I turned to see him pulling out three red velvet cupcakes. The poor guy just couldn't get out of his own way.

"So, what about Mystery Woman?" Felix asked. "When did she get here?"

"She was here when I walked in, so before two. And she's been doing exactly what she did yesterday. Just sitting, writing, and sipping."

"That's weird," I admitted in a whisper. "I mean, this isn't a great spot or anything. And the view stinks. Has she talked to anyone?"

"Just when she asks for more water. But to be fair, who would she talk to? Austin?"

At that point, Austin approached the table with three drip coffees and the red velvet cupcakes. We took them without complaint. It wouldn't do a bit of good, so why bother?

As we ate the moist, red cakes, our talk turned far more trivial. Darcy would be going to a soccer game the next day and invited us to join her. Felix brought up the visit his twin sister, Alex, planned to make in October. I asked what they thought I should do about Ashley. It was our general daily chit chat.

At the end of Darcy's break she went back to shelving new books. Felix and I grabbed a checker game from the stack in the corner and played a few rounds. I wasn't into it and lost each time. While Felix realized I wasn't giving it my all, he still

51

eagerly waved his championships in my face.

After about an hour, our mystery woman pushed her empty cup to the other side of the table, closed her brown leather notebook, and put away her pen. Grabbing her purse, she got up from the table. I figured she was heading to the rest room since she left her leather journal behind. Surely anyone who would write for hours wouldn't forget her notebook.

"Hey, Felix, look. She left her journal."

"Nah, she must be coming back. She was fixated on it. She wouldn't forget it."

"I'm going to see if she's in the women's room. Maybe she's coming back."

Walking in, I checked under the stall doors for feet. No one. I was alone or she was standing on a toilet. If she was, I probably didn't want to know why.

I returned to our table and Felix had the book in hand.

"What're you doing? What if she's in the stacks?"

"She isn't. Darcy said she left about ten minutes ago. I just wanted to clear it from the table before Austin threw it out or something." He flipped through the pages and scowled. "What the hell? There's nothing in it."

"What?" I said, grabbing the notebook, running my fingers along the worn, chocolatey brown leather. "Nothing in it?" Opening it to the middle, I wondered what Felix was talking about. The journal was full of the same finely written script as was on the box in my room.

5

"OKAY, SO FOUR of us have tried, and you're the only one who can read the damn thing," Felix said, flipping through the journal. Before we left Turn the Page, he tried a few different times to read it, as did Darcy, Starr, and her boyfriend, Leon. Now, Felix and I sat next to each other on my bed discussing the situation.

"I get that, and yes, it's insane. But what might be even weirder is the stuff she recorded in this 'invisible' writing. Listen to this. 'I, Fallon Airleas Sterling, do hereby entrust this grimoire to Clan Cassidy. May the wise mother bestow this book and all that is does contain upon the heir of Cassidy, she who shall be kept and the great force outside the pentagram.' What the hell is that?"

"Airleas? Really? That's unflattering."

"Her middle name? That's what you're stuck on?" I rolled my eyes, making sure he saw me. "This chick's journal is invisible to everyone but me. She bestows the book upon some clan. She mentions a pentagram. Dude, there are some huge issues here, and not one of them is her middle name."

Sometimes this guy was exasperating and I wondered why we hung out at all. Besides, I actually liked the name Airleas. It was different. Gaelic I figured. Maybe I'd name a cat that one day.

"Okay, okay. Sure, there are some weird things here."

"Weird? Whatever. You're insane if you think this is merely weird. The woman is a mess. She's crazy."

"Keep reading," he said, his interest focused on me and the book.

"It gets kind of sing-songy as it goes. It's like it isn't her voice anymore. 'The heir shall take the rule of three, double it back, and easily see. Beyond the light, within the soul, the heir of Cassidy shall control; darkness, night, and daylight, bind, protector of all humankind.' "

Felix's expression changed, a look of concern showing clearly.

"What? What is it?"

" 'The protector of all humankind'? That's doesn't freak you out? What if this is you, Liza? Are you seriously ready to protect all humans?"

"It's not me. This is just stupid. I find a book and suddenly I'm Supergirl? Don't even tell me you believe any of this."

"You may not, but I do. I know the rule of three. My abuelita talks about it all the time. Whatever you do comes back threefold. If you send out positive energy, it comes back multiplied by three. If you send out negative energy, well, watch out. No one needs that."

"Okay, so I've heard that, just like karma and all that. But the rest? Really?"

"I don't know." He shook his head as he thought. "There is stuff out there we don't understand. Ya know?"

"And aliens and government conspiracies, too, right?"

Felix reached over and turned on my game console.

"Seriously?" I asked. "This is just not the time to play."

"Not play, Liza. Research."

Honestly confused, I stared at him with the same look all college students give a professor when they "review" things we've never heard of before. Nothing makes us panic the same way as learning something for the first time that the teachers swears we should already know.

"Research what? I have no clue what you're talking about."

He grabbed the blank case of the *The Midnight Witches* game and finally light dawned. If the game was in a box with Fallon's visible writing, maybe they were tied together.

"Oh, my God! Why didn't I think of that?"

"That's why I'm here, lovey. So, let's see what this crazy game means? You in?"

"I'm in." I grabbed my beanbag and threw it down next to the desk chair Felix had wheeled over. Controller in hand, I was ready to figure it all out.

The game started the same way as before, a pan of the

56

town's square, the fog, and the tree. I kept watching for the close-up of Margaret, but it didn't show. Instead, we were shown a red-headed woman as she took off through the crowd. She didn't look like Margaret at all. We were led to the same woods I had seen before, but this time, no one called out her name. Instead there were sounds of the mob as they raced to the woods. The woman disappeared, and we did exactly what I'd done the night before. We ran down paths, crossed bridges. I saw the same small cottage, but it was merely background. There was no secret path leading to it.

"That's the house. There, on the right. That's where Margaret was," I explained to Felix.

"I can't even turn that direction," he said. "Maybe there's a cheat code or something."

"No, I just walked over. But it's all different this time."

"This is getting damn strange. I've seen games change, but normally they don't alter this drastically."

"If I can't get to her house, I can't talk to her. Last time she said I had a journey. She said it wasn't a good time for our kind. She made me tea. But now...now nothing. What is going on, Felix? This is making me feel crazy. I faint and then all of this. What the hell?"

"It's gonna be all right. You aren't dizzy or anything right now, are you? You feel okay, right?"

"Yeah, I'm fine. I just—" I looked up at the game to see

57

Margaret in the corner of the screen. She was part of the mob that appeared as we changed levels. "Look! Look! Right there, in the bottom right. The woman staring at us. That's her!"

Felix turned his gaze toward her just quickly enough to catch the image before it became part of the general crowd again.

"There? The pale woman with dark hair?" He pointed to the corner.

"Yes, that's her. That's Margaret."

"That's not Margaret, Liza. That's, well, you know who that is, don't you?"

"What do you mean? That's Margaret."

"No, Liza, it's not. It's Doctor Drummond."

"Thank you for calling the office of Doctor Julia Drummond. How can I help you?" The voice of an older woman chimed happily as she answered the phone.

"Oh, wow, sorry. I just thought I'd get a machine or something." This was not starting off well. I took a deep breath and tried again. "Hi, I saw Doctor Drummond last night."

"Not a problem, hon. I get that reaction a lot. Not too many offices answer on Sunday afternoons. So, how can I help you, Liza?"

"I saw Doctor Drummond in the ER. She gave me her office number in case—wait, how did you know my name?"

The woman stammered a bit, finally answering, "Oh, um, well, caller ID. Yes, your name appeared on my caller ID. That's all."

"Oh, okay. Sorry about that. Well, Doctor Drummond told me to call if I needed to. Is she in the office today?"

"No, not today. However, she left word that you may call. She'll want to see you. Are you available to meet her in about an hour?

"Sure. At the hospital?"

"Oh, certainly not. Not today. Java Joe's?"

It sounded odd, having a medical consult at a coffee shop, but I supposed it was par for the very odd course I was playing. "On Broad Street? Yeah, I can do that. Thank you."

"Not a problem. I'll let her know. Have a lovely afternoon."

Hanging up my cell phone, I replayed the short conversation in my head.

"So, where are we headed?" Felix asked, breaking me out of my thoughts.

"Java Joe's. In about an hour. I figure we'll just take the T."

"Maybe we can hit Faneuil Hall? Please, please."

59

Felix loved all the tourist trappings of Boston. I loved them too. Most people pretend to hate the local tourist hot spots. Maybe they do hate them after repeated field trips in school and fighting with out-of-towners to enjoy their local treasures. I didn't care how many people were there, though. I love the historical elements of Boston, of all of New England. And Faneuil Hall is a favorite. I never told Felix how much I love the bustle of people in the marketplace, so he felt the need to beg for my participation the same way he did when he wanted to go to the aquarium or visit the Constitution. He didn't need to, but I wasn't about to share that with him. It was one of the only things I had on him.

The historic marketplace includes four separate areas. It was built in the mid-1700s and redone in the 1970s. Where livestock and staple items were once sold, now stood bars and stores selling Boston knickknacks. They also have a huge food court. It's like a mall, but way better. Granted, there are plenty of spots catering to the out-of-towners, but the juxtaposition of history and pop culture lures me, and I go every chance I get.

"I guess so. If you want to deal with all the people and whatever." I turned from him and smiled. I hadn't been to the spot in a few months and was eager to get back too.

As we rode the T to our meeting with Doctor Drummond, Felix started analyzing the last few days.

"Ya know, Liza, I have a little experience with freaky stuff, but this is so bizarre." He was referring to his twin sister, Alejandra's, experiences as a medium. Apparently, she found out about her special ability on their fifteenth birthday, but it wasn't just any ghost that reached out to her. It was their mom. Maybe that's why Felix and I got on so well. We both had MIA mothers. His had died when they were young, and mine might have died too. Even if she was alive somewhere, she was dead to me. Kind of the same thing.

"I don't think this is quite the same. No one is asking me to deliver messages to their family from across the great divide or anything."

"Not yet," he said. He was right. The day was still opening to us and it became more obvious every minute that anything could happen. As my grandmother used to say over and over in her thick Boston accent, "Ya nevah know."

"Well, let's hope we don't go down that road. I can't imagine how annoying that must be. People, I mean ghosts, just popping up whenever they want to."

"Alex has gotten used to it. At first, she freaked out every time one came through to her. But now she just asks them to wait. I think she has some kind of mental take-a-number wheel like at the deli."

The thought of it made us both laugh. I could see ghosts sitting on the other side taking a number from the big red wheel, waiting for their number to be shown on a digital board. Now serving number 117. Anyone? Anyone?

"Isn't it weird to think that your sister talks to ghosts?"

"It was at the beginning. But now I know she lives in two worlds, ours and the spirit world. She's lucky really. She isn't scared of death the way the rest of us are. She already knows what's going to happen. And she knows that if she needs to talk to someone in this world once she's crossed over, she can. That's kind of cool really."

"I guess so. But I still hope that doesn't happen to me." I blanched at the thought of it. I don't know why it bothered me so much to think of communicating with the dead. Maybe it's because I had enough problems communicating with the living.

"Well, something's going on. I just hope Drummond can tell us what it is."

"Me too, Feel. Me too."

We both spent some time looking out the train windows. In Boston, much of the subway system isn't actually underground. Instead, the trains run both above and below ground, so you'll come out of a tunnel and into the sunshine. It isn't always the best view, but I love our city and I love seeing different parts of it. Even the skankier bits.

As the T came to a screeching halt, the echo of metal on metal sounding through the fresh air, we pushed our way out into the fall afternoon.

"Did you tell her I was coming?" Felix asked.

"No. Crap. Well, if she doesn't want you there, you can go hang out next door. I heard Tiles is having a sale."

The record shop was one of the first places I took Felix. He told me about his vinyl fetish—his words, not mine—as he poured through the small batch of records I had in my dorm room. Tiles had the good stuff too. They had tons of vintage vinyl and plenty of new stuff. Their walls were lined with CD cases, and in the age of digital downloads, those were almost antique in their own right.

"Hell, I may ditch you with the doc and go over anyway."

My suggestion piqued his interest, but I hoped he'd stay with me. I had a feeling I wasn't going to want to hear what Doctor Drummond had to say by myself.

It was a short walk to Java Joe's from the T, by design I suppose. Nowhere better to put a coffee shop than on a direct route to and from a transit stop. And this particular shop had a great New England vibe. It served fresh drip coffee from fair trade beans and organic dairy and soy products, but it was decorated with Bostonian sarcasm. Signs reading things like "Mass-hole" and "Screw the Yankees" hung on the walls. T-shirts and sport memorabilia were framed and hung as art. You could see a signed picture of the Celtics circa 1984 hanging next to a green T-shirt reading "Cow Hampshire." The owners definitely knew their customer base and played to them well.

Walking into the shop, I panned the room seeking out the woman whom I hoped would answer some of our questions. Not seeing her amid the group of afternoon coffee enthusiasts wearing Patriots T-shirts and Harvard logos, Felix and I ordered and sat near the window where we would be sure to see her enter. I sipped my large, hot, dirty chia tea latte and realized how pretentious my order actually was. Granted, Felix had outdone me, as always, with his iced, skinny hazelnut macchiato, sugar-free syrup, extra shot, light ice, no whip.

We probably looked like two average college students in our Sunday not-so-bests. My jeans had worn spots on both knees and my T-shirt had at least one small tear. Felix fared better in skinny jeans and a super great fedora but still wasn't dressed to his usual standards. Little did anyone know what we'd been up against in the last eighteen hours or so. But since we didn't really know what we had dealt with, maybe the confusion and anticipation showed through as eagerness or excitement rather than anxiety.

"So, do you think Greeks hand down their good china?" Felix asked out of nowhere.

"What? What are you talking about?"

"They're constantly throwing them on the ground and smashing them. Yelling 'Opa' and all that."

Finally catching on, I answered. "Now that I think about

it, well, maybe. I mean, they can't break all the dishes, right?"

I laughed at my friend and his interesting way of considering the world. The bell over the front entrance tinkled quietly
and Felix sat up straighter. That meant one of two things.
Either the doctor had arrived or someone gorgeous and male
had just walked in.

I turned my head and saw the face of the woman in the
game, Doctor Julia Drummond.

6

"I DON'T THINK I understand. That just sounds, well, it sounds totally ridiculous," I said, my voice getting higher pitched. My nervous voice. I was clearly stressed out. Nothing she said made sense to me.

"Actually, Liza, it does kind of make sense," Felix added.

How did any of this make sense to him? Who was he kidding all of a sudden?

"If you think about it. The story is plausible."

"What the hell is plausible here? Seriously, are you two just screwing with me? For the love!"

"Liza, I promise. I am not doing this to you. This was done hundreds of years ago, and it doesn't merely affect you. You'll notice that I'm a part of all of this too."

Doctor Drummond—Julia—began to explain herself again, slowly. Patience oozed out of this woman. No wonder she was such a great doctor.

"During the 1600s, the settlers of this area—"

"The Puritans, right?"

"Jeez, Felix, shut up. I'm having a hard enough time following any of this without you chiming in."

"Don't worry, Doc. She gets a little testy from time to time. Is that a witch thing?"

Julia laughed, reminding me of the bell that chimed when she entered. It was a light, easy laugh. We obviously didn't feel the same way about this information. If I laughed, I feared it would sound like the cackle of an asylum resident.

Oh, great. Cackle. I was already living up to her story.

"Well, maybe. But I think it is more of a 'she just got life-changing information' kind of thing."

"Okay, can we all stop talking about me like I've left the room? It feels like I'm insane already. I don't need you guys doing this too."

"I'm sorry, Liza. I know how you feel. I found out just a few years ago and it shook me up too. So, let me go over it again. In the mid-1600s, the witch trials started."

"Yeah, I know. In Salem with the burning and all that," I said urging her to continue.

"Well, no actually. The first witches were tried here in Boston and they were hanged. So were the women in Salem. All but one, that is. She was pressed to death."

Disgust crossed Felix's face. "Pressed? Oh, my God!"

I couldn't bring myself to say anything. The idea of someone being flattened between boards or rocks or whatever horrified me, especially since I didn't know if what Julia was about to say meant that same thing could happen to me.

"But that had little to do with what we need to discuss really. Basically, you need to know about Margaret….Margaret Swanson."

"Margaret?" I asked with wide eyes. "The woman in the game? Who is she?"

"Was she," Julia corrected. "She was a midwife tried as a witch, the first person to die in the colonial witch trials. They found her guilty and hanged her."

"Was she a witch?"

"As a matter of fact, no. That's where history had it all wrong."

"So," Felix said, "there were no witches?"

"Of course there were witches. Margaret Swanson just wasn't one of them. In fact, none of the women found guilty were witches. And there were a few men tried here and there, but they weren't witches either."

"So, the big story is that people who weren't witches were tried, found guilty, and died? Everyone already knew that." Annoyed, I started getting restless and a little snippy.

"That's what everyone knows, but it's only part of the truth."

I nodded for her to continue. This is why I was here. This is what I needed to know about.

"Well, Margaret was a keeper. The Puritans killed keepers and left the witches alone. They didn't realize it, of course, but that's what they did."

Confused, I broke my short-lived silence. "What's a keeper?"

"Oh, wow, you didn't get very far in the game I guess. Where did you stop exactly?"

"Margaret was telling me what a bad time it was for our kind. I didn't know what she meant or who she was. She said I had a journey."

"That you do. But now I'm wondering how you decided to call me if you didn't get the direction to do so."

"Because the chick in the game looks just like you. That's why she called. We played today and the woman was your identical twin in old timey clothes," Felix explained for me.

"I forgot about that part. That's so odd even to me. I forget the resemblance sometimes. So, you saw her and called because we look alike? Did anything else happen?"

"Well, I found this book. It belongs to Fallon Sterling. I can read it, but Felix can't."

"So, the long-lost Fallon came out to play. Well, you must be important, Liza. Very important."

"What does that mean? Who's Fallon, and what's a keeper?"

"I'm sorry, it seems we need to cover more than I originally thought. It's going to take some time. Do you guys have anything else you need to do today?"

"Not anymore," I said. "I'm not going anywhere until I hear what all of this means."

"Great. Where were we?"

We all settled in with our drinks and ordered some cinnamon churros. Nothing goes better with life-altering news than fried food after all.

"You didn't mention keepers the first time. You just said I'm a witch."

"You are. And witches have keepers." How she kept her pleasant demeanor while talking about all of this shocked me. But, I didn't know what was coming next and she did. Maybe that was the difference.

Felix couldn't sit still for very long on a good day, so it was no shock that he interjected again. "Witches like wiccans or pagans? Witches like that?"

"Not exactly. Liza, you're a witch by birth, not religion. Most of our kind had a religion outside of their birth craft, so if you have one, there's no need to abandon it or anything."

"Oh, great. I can stay Catholic. That's the thing I like least about my family. Irish-Scottish Catholic. How original."

"Well, you can add witch now. That ought to spice things up a bit," Felix said with a smile. He probably enjoyed not being the only one with a freak show for a family tree.

"You are a witch. In fact, you're a witch along the Cassidy line."

"That's what Fallon's journal said. It said it had to be read by the heir of Clan Cassidy. That's me?"

"Yes, that's you. The heir of Clan Cassidy, and a witch. And each witch has a keeper."

"Is that you?" I asked with some hope. I still wasn't sure what a keeper was, but I figured it was better to have one I knew than one I didn't.

"No. Fallon, the woman with the journal, I'm her keeper actually. We've had a falling out recently is all. But I'm glad to see she reached out to you. You, at the moment, are keeperless. That's part of the issue we have here. All witches must have a keeper, and you...well, don't. But you will. We just have to find her."

"Why? What will she do?"

"A keeper watches over and protects her witch. Most of us have some kind of modern medical training now. But with the Puritans, keepers were botanists of sorts. The fact that they treated people with herbs and brews was enough to create the suspicion of witchcraft. Ultimately, the keepers were the ones tried and killed, and the witches remained protected. They carried on in the community, raised their children, and remained productive women in society."

"Okay, so I'm a witch. Was my mother? I mean, how am I related to this clan? Where are they from?"

"Some of that I don't know, but you'll find out along the

way. You are a witch, by birth, meaning at least one of your parents has witch blood. If you are Clan Cassidy, then your witch blood goes back to the old country, to what is now Ireland and witch royalty really."

"Queen of the witches. I love it!" Felix was probably thinking more about rhyming witches with something else.

"Could be, actually," Julia said with a shoulder shrug. "Since you aren't my witch, I don't have all of the details on you. But Cassidy blood is important in our circles, Liza. That means you're important. And that means we need to find your keeper fast."

"What happens if we don't? Find my keeper, I mean."

"Well, that isn't something I really want to get into right now. Besides, we'll find her. She just needs to get the call. They all show eventually."

She didn't sound as convincing as I'd hoped, but I had too many questions to get hung up on sure and certain death, or whatever I had coming my way.

"So, as a witch, what do I do? I don't know spells or anything."

"You'll learn," she said with a smile. "They all do. And you already have the grimoire."

"The what?" Felix asked.

"The grimoire. It's a book of spells and incantations handed from one witch to another. Fallon made sure you ended up with hers. She's been looking for you for a few years."

She sipped her tea and let me soak everything in. It would take a few rounds at Java Joe's for me to really start to understand, but Julia was good to give me a little time. Even Felix seemed to realize that I needed a minute and kept himself busy looking out the window.

As I gazed, I saw men in business suits and some in jeans, women in high heels carrying designer bags and others chasing small children. A few teenagers listened to headphones, somehow carrying on a conversation at the same time. Green leaves blew past. I found myself focusing more on my reflection and less on the items outside the longer I looked. I waited. I knew it would happen, but I wasn't sure as to when. Then, suddenly, my reflection started changing again, looking wavy like it would on rippling water.

"Liza, Liza, are you all right? Can you hear me?" Julia's voice sounded far away but clear.

I heard her sharp enunciation of each word and wondered where she was from. I wondered, but I didn't ask.

"You try, Felix. Maybe she'll respond to a more familiar voice."

"What do I say?" he asked. His voice showed concern.

"Anything. Just talk to her."

"Hey, Liza? Girl, are you in there? I mean I've seen you go cross-eyed and all, but this is kind of crazy-eyed. Snap out of it."

I thought I was smiling, but I couldn't tell.

Was my face moving at all? Why could I hear them but not answer at all?

I felt myself slumping, falling out of my chair. The wooden floor was surprisingly warm.

"Liza!" Felix rushed to grab my arm, but he was too late. I was splayed across the floor, a position I was becoming far too familiar with.

"She's all right, everyone. She's fine. Just back up. Give her some space."

Julia's commanding voice soothed the vibrations in the room. I could feel the anxiety ease in those who rushed to surround me. They began to back away.

"She's tranced. I thought that might be what happened when you came to Regional last night." She sighed loudly.

"You're shaking your head. That isn't good."

"She'll be fine. It may take a few minutes though. Basically, her magic is working. I tried to get to her before all of this started. Dammit, Fallon. If she'd just worked with me, Liza wouldn't have to go through any of this."

Felix dropped his voice low, sounding serious and sullen. "Doc, what is she going through?" The concern echoing in his question melted my heart.

"Felix, it's a lot to explain, but I promise you, she will

be okay. If she had a keeper, that would help her focus these trances and give her outlets for her magic. For now, this is how it all manifests."

"So, this will keep happening until she finds her keeper?"

"Unfortunately, yes. But the game, playing the game, may help a bit. It will explain some things and help her practice. The more she practices, even without a keeper, the better she'll be able to control her magic."

She knelt behind me, placing my head in her lap.

"But she's powerful, Felix. Maybe more powerful than I realized. These...let's call them seizures...will keep happening until we scout out her keeper. I'm doing my best, but I need information about the witch who left the notebook. Is there anything you can tell me about Fallon?"

"I don't really know anything. We ran into her at Turn the Page, a bookstore by campus. Our friend, Darcy, mentioned her to us and—"

Julia broke in. "Why? Why did she mention Fallon?"

"She just said a woman was sitting in the store all day writing and drinking tea. She didn't look at anything in the store and was dressed for a stakeout. Big glasses and scarf, ya know?"

"That's so Fallon. Leave it to her to call more attention to herself while trying to hide." Frustration crossed her face, reaching her eyes which suddenly looked concerned.

CARRIE L. WELLS

"She sounded like someone you just had to witness, so we went to the store. She was there, writing and sipping, and then she got up and left. And when she did, she left the journal behind. I flipped through it, but there was nothing there. Then Liza looked at it and could read every word."

"Nice. Well, at least she masked the book. But to just leave it there. Good goddess. Not much of a plan there."

She turned back to me, rubbing my temples and humming to me softly. The crowd of customers didn't seem to notice me anymore and I wondered how long I'd been on the floor.

"It looks like she's coming around. She'll be thirsty. Can you go get her some water? Or juice? Juice would be better."

Felix made his way past me to the front counter. Julia took the time alone with me to bend to my ear and said, "Liza. Honey, I need you to focus. Listen to my voice and open your eyes when you're ready. Let the darkness clear. Shake it away. You can do this. You're powerful. You don't need to let this take over. You can move past it. Go ahead, try."

I blinked my eyes slowly, and I felt the haze that closed in begin to move away. The coffee shop came into focus and I watched Felix's sidewinders make their way to our table. Julia helped me sit up and take a few sips of freshly squeezed orange juice. The sugar immediately hit me and I felt dizzy all over again.

76

Supported by Julia, I breathed slowly and gave myself a little time to reconnect with my surroundings.

"Welcome back!" Felix seemed caught between sarcasm and sheer joy. I must have truly scared his scrawny butt.

I moved to get up, wobbling slightly as Julia helped me.

"Take it slow, speedy. No rush here. How ya feeling?"

"I'm all right, I think. How long was I down?"

Julia glanced at the large Salvador Dali-esque wall clock that appeared to be melting but could still tell the correct time.

"About twenty-five minutes or so this time. Nothing too crazy, but you were obviously tranced. You could hear us, couldn't you?"

"Yep, every word." I paused to catch my breath and look around. "So, all of this will stop when we find my keeper?"

"It should. She'll help you let some of this excess energy out. It takes over your vision at times, and if you aren't careful, it can happen more frequently."

"So, what do I do? I can't let this keep happening. If nothing else, I'm getting way too familiar with wicked dirty floors."

Felix choked back a garbled laugh. I'm sure it was quite a sight to see me sprawled on yet another business's floor, but I was lucky enough to have him with me each time it had happened.

"Wait," I said with too much zeal. "Is there anything that

77

can worsen…I mean, anything that would intensify my reactions?"

"You mean like a catalyst? Something to send your magic out of control?"

"Yea, exactly. Is there?"

"Sometimes conflicting magic will make things a little worse."

"Conflicting magic?" Felix asked. "What's that?"

"Well, there are various magical realms. Each works in its own system. And some of them don't play well together," Julia explained. "Is there anyone else magical in your life? Is there someone you would suspect perhaps?"

Felix and I turned to one another and sighed.

"Me. I might be," Felix confessed. "My sister is a medium. I guess our mother was a *bruja* and so was our grandmother."

"Hmmm. Mexican magic, huh?"

"Si, that's the Montoya way." He flashed his brilliant smile at her, but you could tell he was worried.

"Well, it isn't the most compatible magical form, but it isn't dark magic by any means. It's just a bit different. That shouldn't do much."

"Oh, good. See, Feel, you can't get rid of me just because Alex talks to dumb ol' ghosts." Finally happy about some of Julia's news, I smiled with my entire face. I'd hate to take any of this head-on without Felix.

"Okay, great," he said with less than complete conviction. "That's great. We won't let her stuff get in our way."

Julia felt his hesitation, as did I. But she called him on it. "Felix, is there something else?"

"Well, just something small, really."

My smile faded as I questioned what information would come next.

"What is it? What small thing is it, Felix? Seriously, spit it out already."

"Uh, well, I kind of…" His voice trailed off.

Julia, as encouragement, explained, "You can't take me by surprise. I'm a keeper and a doctor. What I haven't seen or heard in one role, I have in the other."

"Well, I'm a shifter. There. That's it."

Julia gasped loudly, obviously surprised. I had no idea what he was talking about, so it left me unphased.

"Is that like a swinger?" I asked seriously.

"No, Liza. It's not," Julia said with a small laugh. "He's a shape shifter."

"What the hell is that?"

"I…don't laugh. Promise you won't laugh?" His cheeks flushed and his embarrassment was clear.

"I don't know what I'd be laughing at, so go ahead. Spit. It. Out."

He gulped audibly. "I turn into a cat."

I couldn't help it. I laughed.

7

"FELIX THE CAT? Are you kidding me?"

He wasn't, but I figured I'd ask anyway. I just couldn't let it pass.

"Yes, yes, yes. For a million times, yes. Felix, the freaking fracking cat. Will you stop laughing already?"

Apparently, he was over my delight at his ridiculous news. But I had just heard my BFF turned from gay guy to *gato*. Who wouldn't laugh?

"Okay, okay. I'll try. I'm sorry. I just didn't expect that news. I mean, after finding out about the witch stuff and the trances. And now you're a cat."

"Well, I'm not always a cat, obviously. I'm very much not a cat right now."

"Are you sure? I mean I've always thought you were one cool cat."

I broke into hysterics again. It was a much needed release and once I started laughing like that, I had a hard time stopping. Tears fell from my eyes and my side cramped while my laugh deepened. It was an extreme reaction to his announcement, but the emotions needed to come out in one form or another. Laughter it was. Eventually, I went from my normal laugh to snorting. That's when Felix went from trying to ignore me to actually ignoring me. I'd hurt his feelings.

"Oh, I'm sorry, Feel. It's been a long few days and I haven't slept much. You heard what Julia told me. I'm a witch, you're a cat. Life is damn funny right now if you ask me."

"Oh, my head! You're a witch and not only am I a cat, I'm a black cat. Crap!"

That sent me into hysterics all over again. A witch and a black cat. What a pair we were.

"Okay, so when do you…you know, change? At the full moon or something?"

I'd never seen his feline form, so obviously he switched at will or when we weren't together.

"Uh, no," he said in the tone of a frustrated teenager. "Nothing that cliché. I can change when I want to now."

"Now?"

"Yeah, the first year or so it would just happen. Add that to the horrors of being a gay Hispanic male and your little discovery today seems far less upsetting by comparison. Well, at least in my book."

I pouted and rolled my eyes. He was probably right, but it surely wasn't what I wanted to hear. I was still mid pity party, and I wanted it to continue.

"Thanks. One bright spot, no random cat hair in my room. I'll cherish this silver lining."

"Stop being so bitchy," he snapped at me. "Seriously. You're a witch. You got dizzy. That doesn't mean anything really. Even Julia said that you won't have to change your life much."

"So she says. But really, what the hell? This is too much. I have some keeper who will miraculously show up one day. That won't change my life at all, right? And don't forget the mystery lady leaving me a book in invisible writing. Oh, and a game that will teach me to harness my magic. What the hell? The universe hates me. It just hates me so freaking bad!"

"Well, maybe Julia was right. Maybe we were drawn together because of our magic. That would explain a lot, right? And that's pretty awesome."

"Wicked awesome," I corrected smiling.

"Right. That's wicked awesome. So, if we're both magical, let it be. Bring it on, universe." He took my hand and raised it up like I had just won a boxing match.

Leave it to Felix to fixate suddenly on the sentimental aspects of our new identities. He sounded confident, but I remained scared and skeptical.

"Maybe. But I'm not convinced."

Julia had explained that I needed to spend time with the grimoire and the game. She plugged her number into my cell phone and told me to call any time I needed her. Then she asked me to give it to Fallon if I ran into her and she had a feeling I would, soon.

Apparently, I could expect to keep trancing frequently. She told me to start practicing some and suggested that I get back to my dorm and read through the journal. That was the only way to channel the magic that would eventually take me over if it wasn't released.

"I don't like the sound of that," I'd told her when she cautioned me.

"You shouldn't. It's not a good thing. Practice, Liza. It will help. And without a keeper, that's all I can suggest."

"So, do I just follow a spell? Just pick one and try it out?"

"You can. You won't be drawn to anything that you can't handle. That's the glory of magic. Actually, you may not be able to find spells that are too much for you. Fallon probably hid them. She's smart like that.

"Better yet, the grimoire may choose spells for you. If you can complete them, you'll have released at least a little of your power."

"Hid them? How? Are they somewhere else?"

"No, hid as in cloaked. She's a witch, after all. She can do things like that, and eventually you'll be able to as well. Just you wait."

Okay, so that sounded cool. Maybe not worth the disruption and shock, but cool. At least it would keep Ashley out of my stuff.

"Doesn't she need a wand or cauldron or something like that?" asked Felix with a sarcastic edge. He had a clear vision of a witch in his head and I don't think I matched it well.

"No, nothing like that." Julia laughed at our ignorance. I'm sure it was sweet to her that we had such little understanding of her world. My world. "But she will need to focus. Do you have a roommate?"

I groaned. Just the thought of Ashley made my head hurt. "Yes, I do. She's at the Beta Zeta house more often than not though. That's why she's still alive."

"Well, take advantage of your time alone and focus your energy. Then read the grimoire. Consider what pulls at you, what grabs at your core. Read it over and over. Read it so many times that you find yourself chanting it like a song. But before you do, go through more of the game. It will help. I promise you, at the hand of the mother, it will help."

"That's intense." Felix said exactly what I thought.

Julia took both my hands in hers. Warmth and comfort enveloped my entire body and I felt a sudden easiness. Calm took over my frustration and anxiety. Was that a keeper thing?

Looking directly into my eyes, she said, "You're special, Liza, even in our circles. I can't explain more than that, but you are. Take care of yourself and practice. And when you see Fallon, please let her know where I am. It's important."

"I will. If I see her."

"You will, and soon." She turned sharply and walked away.

"That was kind of abrupt."

"She's a busy woman, Liza. A doctor and a keeper. Whatever that is."

"Why do I have a feeling that we'll know all about it soon enough?"

Having finally ditched Felix, I stood outside the door to my room. Silence filled the space between normal background noises of laughter and television voices on the third floor of Flanagan Hall. I crossed my fingers and wished for Ashley to be gone. I didn't need to deal with her right now. Just the thought of her was giving me a headache.

I opened the door slowly, hoping to keep the squeaky hinges quiet. Sticking my head inside, I thought of the murderer in Poe's "The Tell-Tale Heart," the crazy who waited outside the door of his victim's room for nights, waiting to catch him awake. Maybe my motivation wasn't the same, but my movements were. I eased myself into the room, trying to let the sleeping dog lie if she was lying at all.

Finally getting into my room, I saw the curtains opened

wide, her bed made, and the floor littered with clothes. Nothing like I left it that morning. But, even if it was a mess, it was empty. Empty and quiet. Empty, quiet, and my own personal oasis.

I climbed into my bed, not to read or think, but to hug my stuffed monkey, Lobo. It's ridiculous, but even in college I find myself grabbing for my childhood toy when I need comfort. The stuffed animal had bare spots where I had either matted or pulled off sections of its fleecy covering. My grandmother, a top notch toy surgeon, had sewn his left ear back on not once, but twice, and fixed his embroidered mouth which had been red but paled to pink. And while I wouldn't admit it to Felix, Lobo was my best friend.

Hugging the monkey to my chest, I caved into the hollow feeling I'd fought back for the last few hours. I knew I should take the time alone to look at the game or the book, but I choose to look at the inside of my eyelids. My life went topsy-turvy in mere hours, and I could do absolutely nothing about it. It hit me in waves, and the biggest one yet pulled me under.

An hour later I woke with a humming in my ears like a vibrating cell phone. Looking around, I found nothing that would make such a noise, but it remained persistent. While the volume didn't change, the speed of it did. The reverberations came closer together as I approached Fallon's journal. The damn thing buzzed audibly as I reached out to grab it. Julia said it would call to me, but I didn't expect it to actually make noise. I wondered if only I could hear it since I was the only one who could read it.

With the crazy, vibrating book in hand, I made my way to my beanbag. I flopped down ungracefully. I flipped through the first few pages and skipped to the middle. The book, however, had different ideas and suddenly pages were turning without my help to page 42. I shut it and opened it again. Page 42. I turned to the last pages. They flipped again. Page 42.

"Okay," I said loudly. "I'll read it."

Obviously, I had a grimoire with control issues.

"Page 42. Cloaking," I read. " 'I call upon the cloak of night to hide this item in plain sight.' Use this spell to hide common household items by averting others from their notice. With your palm flat, facing the object, circle clockwise three times over the item you wish to hide. Repeat the title incantation once for every circle of your hand. Others will see the item, but it will not register as important."

I got the idea that maybe I should use this spell on the book itself. It made sense. If I were a magic book, the first thing I'd do is ensure my own safety, especially if I knew I would be residing in the same room as crazy Ashley.

Standing and placing the book on my desk, I attempted the spell. "I call upon the cloak of night to hide this item—

Ouch!" My fingers tingled with sparks of pain and I could see a pale blue light. My fingertips flashed and shot tiny bursts of lightening over the book which opened back to page 42. It urged me to complete the spell.

"Fine. I'll try it again. But be nice," I said sternly to the grimoire. "I call upon the cloak of night to hide this item in plain sight." The book sat quietly as the blue electricity ran from my hand to its cover. I repeated the circle and the incantation two more times, but nothing grand happened. The light subsided and the book sat still. I supposed I'd need someone else to look at it in order to see if the spell worked.

Picking it up again, the book opened to page 71 this time, "The Pentagram." Here, Fallon had explained in intricate detail the history of the pentagram. She called it the symbol of our legacy and went over the five points and the myriad of meanings they held. They represented the five senses, the five stages of life, even the five points of the human body. Fallon focused on a different meaning, however. The five elements: spirit, earth, air, water, and fire. She explained that the circle containing the pentagram protected the drawer and connected the elements, showing that they not only relate to each other but also touch and influence once another. Fire can be moved and fed by air. It can be squelched by water. It can be lit in spirit. It can alter earth. The relationship between the elements was unbreakable and constant, yet forever changing, flexing.

What garnered my attention, however, and what struck me, was her mention of the element beyond the pentagram. She said the same thing in her inscription. The element beyond the pentagram. Why didn't she just say what it was? Before I read the grimoire, I thought there were four elements. Spirit wasn't one that I'd ever thought of. Guess I was wrong. Now there was apparently a sixth.

Knock, knock.

I jumped at the noise and the book crashed to the floor unceremoniously. I was sure that was not how I should treat a super-secret, magical manual. I grabbed it and placed it on my desk, then I went to the door. I wondered who it would be. Darcy was at work. Ashley wouldn't knock, and Felix would have squawked that I wasn't at the door already.

Knock, knock, knock.

"Coming. Hold on."

Feeling rushed, I didn't bother to check who it was and opened the door with enough force to send me tripping backward over Ashley's desk chair.

"Oh, man, are you okay?" a male voice asked before I could look up to see its owner.

"Nah, I'm all—oh, hi." I clamored to my feet, dusting myself off and righting the chair, all while staring into the eyes of Fathom.

"Hi. I just, well, I just wanted to, um, well…" He stumbled over his sentence a little and I wondered to myself, *Is he nervous? What the heck?*

"Can I come, I mean, well, God. Can I come in?"

"Sure," I said, backing up again, but this time watching out for the chair. "Come on in."

I wasn't sure what to do with the door, so I let it shut on its own. Propping it open seemed like it was more awkward than polite. If he didn't want to sit in my room, he wouldn't have asked to come in, right?

"Your roommate here?" he asked.

"Nope. I'm not sure where she is. Wait. Are you here to see her?"

"Oh, no. I just, no. No, I came to see you."

At a loss for how to keep the conversation going, I spoke without thinking too hard. "Well, here I am. Take a look." Apparently my plan for this meeting was to open my mouth and let lame, stupid comments fly out. Lovely.

"Yep, there you are. And you're all right? I mean you said you were this morning, but really, you're okay?"

"That I am. Got the all clear from the doctor last night. Just a little dehydrated," I explained figuring that was the next question.

"My roommate was dehydrated so badly last year that he was puking everywhere. Couldn't keep anything down. It was wicked awful. Seriously gross. He would move and hurl, roll over in bed and puke. Oh, crap. I just totally disgusted you. I'm sorry. I guess I didn't need to explain all that."

It intrigued me to see him off his game like this. Every time I'd seen him before, he'd sounded polished and normal. Now he sounded more like me, a blundering idiot. It was endearing, really. Guys didn't usually act that way around me. Generally guys didn't find themselves around me at all.

"So, how did the rest of your night go? I mean you know how I got home, after all." I hoped I sounded a little flirty, but mostly I hoped I made last night sound like it wasn't a big deal.

"I just played some pool and went back to the dorm. Not a big night for me. I figured if I was spilling beer on hot girls before your ambulance ride, I was better off switching to water at that point."

His comment surprised me and his smile left me breathless and smiling too. His teeth lined up like small pearls and I found myself fixated on them. They peeked out from behind lips the perfect shade of pink. They needed to make lipstick that color. Fathom lip pink. I'd buy that and I don't even wear makeup.

"Smart move. Party rule number 1: hydrate. Then you won't need an ambulance too." I tried to laugh without sounding like a giggling Beta Zeta. I failed.

"True, true." He nodded and looked around my room. "Nice place. I'm guessing this is your side," he said, motioning to the colorful quilt on my bed and the Ramones poster hanging on the wall.

His pale green eyes scanned the rest of my room, finally settling on Lobo. Sitting on the bed, he reached for the monkey. He fiddled with the toy and continued to look around.

"Sure is. What gave it away? The absolute lack of style?"

"Sure, if you consider all that Beta Zeta crap a style." He smiled again. I was beginning to like this.

"Nah, I'm no sorority girl. I'm too afraid they'll revoke my friends if my dues are late." I laughed a little, only half kidding.

"Nice. Wicked cynical. I like it." His New England accent pulled apart the word nice and he imbued his statement with sarcasm. This was a Boston boy if I'd ever seen one. But I still didn't understand why he came by. Then again, this seemed to be the weekend for my experiences with the highly unusual.

8

"SO, I TOOK MY sister's favorite Barbie doll, gave it a crew cut, and painted her black, brown, and green. Camo style." Fathom and I laughed at his childhood antics and reached into the chip bag at the same time. His fingertips brushed the back of my hand and goosebumps crawled up my arms.

"You cold?" he asked.

"Uh, yeah, a chill that's all," I lied.

"Did you know that's caused by the contracting of your arrector pili muscles, the little muscles attached to the hair follicles?"

I choked back a small laugh. What an odd thing for this beautiful boy to know. "No. Does anyone but you know that?"

"Okay, probably not. I took an anatomy class in high school, back when I wanted to be a doctor. That always stuck with me."

"A doctor, huh? But not anymore?"

"Nah, I decided that organic chemistry wasn't exactly my friend. Actually, it kicked my ass pretty hard." He chuckled. "But maybe that's because it was at 8:00 a.m. I mean, 8:00 a.m. and I aren't truly friendly either."

"That I can relate to," I said. "I dropped a lit class because it was at eight. I went for a week, and then I bailed. I'm such a slacker." I screwed my face up remembering the guilt I felt when I went to the admissions office to withdraw from the course.

"That's what I hear about you. I mean everyone says it," he jibed.

"What a brat! Are all little brothers like you?" I asked him.

"Yep. We're all alike. No brothers or sisters for you then?"

"Nope. Just me. My parents realized you can't duplicate perfection." I smirked and watched a wide, eye-sparkling smile spread across his face. A real smile. Not the kind that just turns up at the edge of your mouth. A full-face smile.

He didn't need to know the long, ridiculousness of it all, of my father dying and my mother taking off. That's when people realize they don't have the right words anymore. No one knows what to say when you explain that your dad died in a horrible accident when you were three. Then the pity flies across their faces when you get to the part of your mother running off and leaving you with your grandmother.

"It's just me and my sister," he said. "But my mom is one of seven."

"Seven? Jeez! Your grandmother must have been a saint."

"Maybe not for having them, but for raising them." He ran his hand through his hair and shook his head just a bit. "Can you imagine raising seven girls? The prom dresses alone!"

94

"All girls? That's crazy. I can't even imagine coming up with seven names."

"Well, they aren't traditional. I'll give Nana credit for her creativity."

"Creative, huh? Unlike Fathom?"

"My parents definitely followed suit. My sister's name is Carousel, after all."

"That's awesome! How did your folks come up with that?"

"Seriously?" he asked. "You like it?"

"I love it. You guys have the coolest names I've ever heard," I answered truthfully. "They sure beat Elizabeth. Blech." I mimed gagging.

"Elizabeth what? I mean, I know Liza Scott, but what's your middle name?"

"Elizabeth Claire Scott." I said in as regal a voice as my accent would allow. "A proper Irish name."

"That's not bad. But I like Liza better. It suits you."

With that he reached forward and moved a piece of hair out of my eyes, tucking it behind my ear. The intensity of the action had me jumping up, off the bed.

From the other side of the room, as I reached for some sodas, I asked, "So, what are your aunts' names?"

"Are you sure you want to know? You won't think differently about me when I tell you, will you?" I liked his sense of humor. And I liked the smile and deep laugh that went with it.

"Wow, they must be bad. For a guy named Fathom to think his aunts' names will change my opinion of him."

"Ha ha," he said dryly. "Not bad. Different. My mother is Poet, and her sisters are Lark, Journey, Lavynder, Echo, Story, and Fallon."

"Fallon?" My mind immediately ran back to the grimoire. "That's really cool. I mean, they all are. Hey, what's your mom's maiden name?"

If it was an odd question, he didn't appear to notice. "Oh, Sterling. I guess my grandparents figured that with a cool last name like that, they might as well throw out some interesting first names."

"Fallon Sterling? Really?" I paused. "That's your aunt?" How many Fallon Sterling's could there be? She had to be the one, the mystery woman who wrote the grimoire and delivered the game.

"Yeah, do you know her?"

"Not exactly. I've heard the name." Well, he may be my answer to the Fallon question. Maybe now I could find her instead of waiting for her to find me.

"You're into gaming, right?"

How did he know that? Do I have some kind of super cute stalker? Is it weird that I kind of hoped so?

"Yeah, I do some. Why?"

"Then it makes sense you'd have heard her name. She runs Spellcast Gaming up in Revere." His enthusiasm grew as he continued speaking. I could tell he'd just come up with a new idea. "Dude, I should totally have you beta test her new game, *The Midnight Witches*. You'd love it. The art is freaking amazing. You can almost feel the leaves rustle. You in?"

Spellcast Gaming? The name sounded a bit on the nose, but for a witch with a game studio, it made sense.

"Uh, yeah, totally. I'd love to see her stuff. That's what I want to do one day."

"Run a game design company?" he asked.

"Well, not at first, no. I'd love to write the story lines. My buddy, Felix, is a hell of a coder and graphics guy. We plan to team up at some point."

"Awesome. I'll have her send one over to you. She's always looking for testers and complaining that if there were more female-focused games there'd be more female gamers. She'll love you!"

I hoped so. At the very least, I hoped she'd meet me.

We looked at the clock simultaneously, realizing we'd spent hours talking about our favorite bands and hobbies, our majors, and our families. He knew the street I grew up on, and I had been to his uncle's pharmacy more times than I could count.

"Crap, I'm going to be late for hockey practice. I gotta

run, Liza."

"No problem. Glad you came by," I said and realized how very much I meant it. I opened the door to the empty hall and he brushed past me. He was out the door and halfway down the hallway, but he turned and jogged back. Standing almost ten inches taller than my five feet four inches, he cast a shadow over me. Looking up and into his eyes, I could feel my forehead wrinkle unattractively as I thought about his motivation for coming back.

"Did you forget something?" I asked him, confused.

"Yes," he said enthusiastically. He bent down and pressed his lips to mine. It was a quick motion, but purposeful, and I felt the warmth of his breath and his full, strong lips. He pulled away from me and I opened my eyes slowly.

"Okay, now I really gotta go." He smiled at me and took off down the hallway again.

Unconsciously, I brought my fingers to my mouth, touching the spot his lips had lingered. I watched him open the door at the end of the hall and disappear into the stairwell.

Fathom Burke had kissed me. Fathom Freaking Burke!

I wish I had predicted the kiss. I would have prepared to enjoy myself. However, if I was going to be taken by surprise, I hoped Fathom would also be the one to do it.

Two days ago I had no idea the guy even knew my name. Now, after hours of laughing and talking, I knew almost as much about him as I knew about Felix. And, I stood like a dope in my door, too dazed by the experience to walk into my room, I could feel the warmth of his hand on my arm and smell him, or his fabric softener, in the air around me.

Eventually, I did go into my room, thankful Ashley hadn't returned yet. I looked around at the evidence of our time together; an empty bag of chips, some crumbs on my quilt, a couple of soda cans. A *couple* of cans. Maybe that's what we were going to be, a couple. I was obviously smitten. No sane person smiles at soda cans.

My giddiness shifted just a bit as my eyes landed on the grimoire and the game case sitting next to each other. I'd almost forgotten about the strangeness the weekend brought me, choosing to fixate on Fathom instead. But seeing the magical items cleared my head quickly. It was time to get back to business and start playing with my magic.

I tried my hand at spell casting already. Fathom hadn't noticed the book, so it may have even worked. Time to try the game again then. I pulled up my beanbag and popped the game into the console. My controller in hand, I prepped to meet Margaret once again.

The music played, and the same opening scene drew me in. This time the game skipped to Margaret's cottage. No need to walk through the woods or talk to anyone else. Instead, my character sat in the wooden chair inside the stone house. Margaret poured the tea as she had before, but this time I directed my attention to her face. The only difference between her and Julia Drummond was the English accent I heard in her speech. The physical similarity between them was uncanny. I found myself wondering if I looked that much like anyone in my genetic line.

"Oh, Elizabeth, it is such a joy to have you here."

In my head, I answered the woman even though I knew she was ultimately a collection of pixels on a screen. Meanwhile, my character sipped tea I could taste offscreen, and as I thought the words, they were relayed aloud in the game.

"Thank you, Margaret. The tea is delicious." My on-screen self took another sip. "I went to see Julia."

"That's wonderful news. I'm happy you figured out our connection. Fallon believed it would take far longer and you would need some overt directions to meet with Julia before you would do so. I had a differing opinion."

"I actually met Julia last night a few hours before you and I were introduced," I explained. "When I played the game later with Felix, he recognized how much the two of you look alike."

"Ah, it's good you have a magical friend, Elizabeth. Familiars are an important part of a witch's life."

Listening to her, it hit me yet again that I was suddenly a witch.

"What's a familiar?" I asked as a lovely orange and white cat jumped onto the table.

"Oh, Ezra." She reached out to the cat, stroking his head as he nuzzled her. "This is my familiar. My magical companion."

"He's magical?" He looked like a normal cat to me although his fluffy tail reminded me to cat I had as a kid.

"Yes, he is," she said in the high-pitched voice people reserve for babies and animals they adore. "Usually, only witches have familiars, but mine left him with me when she left the village. And he's been very helpful."

"Is Felix my familiar? I mean, he isn't exactly a cat."

"Oh, of course, dear. But he is a familiar all the same. He'll be helpful to you. You will see."

I could feel the heat from her hearth, and the cauldron bubbled over its fire. I listened. Fathom was wrong. I could hear the leaves rustle outside the cottage and the wind circle in the chimney.

Margaret leaned forward a bit, closing the gap between the two of us by about half. She gazed intensely into my eyes.

"Margaret, what are you doing?" I asked. Her eyes were unmoving, not like mine which felt they were darting around the entire room. But since she was so close, it mattered little where I looked. All I saw was her face and it was making me a bit uncomfortable.

101

"Reading, my dear. Just reading." She made no gestures. She didn't move away. She merely continued to stare into my eyes.

I sat still, trying to mimic her gaze. I watched as she looked into my eyes, blinking naturally, and not attempting to have one of those childhood staring contests. Relaxed and calm, she smiled.

I looked into her dark eyes and noticed that they act like a mirror. I'm able to see myself reflected in her corneas and pupils. But if I looked beyond myself, deep into her eyes, it looked like shapes were floating.

"What are you reading? My eyes?"

"Oh, no, child. Not your eyes. Although, they are lovely. Almost the color or amber, aren't they?" She reached out and gently tucked a strand of hair behind my ear. It was the same movement Fathom had made earlier, and it felt just as intimate. However, I didn't jump up this time. This was the action of a mother. The caring, nurturing motion comforted me in this scenario.

"Thank you. My grandmother used to say the same thing. If you aren't reading my eyes, what are you reading?" I asked. Julia had told me to go back into the game to learn and practice. I figured asking questions would help move that process along.

"I'm reading your soul, and if I'm not mistaken, you're

reading mine."

"Your soul? What? I'm not doing that."

"Do you see the swirling shapes behind your reflection? Is your reflection getting hazy, almost like a ripple?"

"Yes, actually," I answered, getting excited. I looked deeper. The shapes began to sparkle, to emit the same pale blue light as my fingertips when I cast the cloaking spell. They glowed like the small fireflies that had shown up in the store window.

"Fascinating, is it not? Watch a little longer and tell me what you see."

The light danced and the shapes drew together and pulled apart.

"I see shapes. They keep changing," I said, trying to wrap my head around the images. "It really doesn't look like much. Just blue, glowing shapes."

"Give it a few minutes. Look to the edges. That is often where it begins."

Looking into her eyes, I waited. I searched the edges of the space. There it was.

"Dragonflies. Wait, no, butterflies. Oh, jeez, everything keeps changing. Now it looks like birds. Are those ravens?" The pieces of light came together to create concentric images shifting from one shape to another. It was like an Escher drawing where the shapes begin as fish and morph to ducks as they progress up the page.

"I don't know." Her voice was jovial, with a lilt of laughter at my fascination. "I cannot read my own soul. Only you can explain what you see."

"I can't. Everything is changing so quickly. What does it all mean? How is this a reading of your soul?"

"The changes represent my changes. How the years have altered my soul and my character. Are they bright or dark?" she asked, guiding me in the reading.

"Bright. There were a few images in shadow, but most are bright and blue. A clear blue light. Almost white."

"A healthy soul I have then. And thank the goddess for it." I could see a smile reflected in the shimmer on the surface of her eyes.

"What do you see, Margaret? In my eyes. What do you see?"

"You are an interesting witch, Elizabeth. Very interesting. But now is not the time to share my reading. It is the time to practice your skills." She finally broke eye contact, easing back a bit and sipping her tea.

"Julia said I should use the game and the grimoire and practice what I'm drawn to."

"And are you? Are you doing that, dear?"

"Yes. I completed a spell today. I used one to shield the book."

"Oh, wonderful. Very smart choice. Did the book assist?"

A little embarrassed, I answered, "Yes, it did. I mean it kept opening to the page. I figured I should try the spell, and I didn't have anything else worthy of cloaking. So I cloaked the book."

"Very wise choice. And it looks like you are open to its direction. That is also a wise choice."

Ezra jumped down from the table and moved closer to the hearth. He circled three times and settled in on the warm stones as Margaret and I watched him.

"Even my cat believes in the power of three," she said lightly. "Did Julia say anything about your keeper?" The tone of her voice shifted. It had a sudden edge to it.

"She said my keeper has yet to show herself."

"And Fallon. Has she said anything?"

"I didn't actually talk to Fallon. She left me the grimoire in a bookstore."

"An entire shop of books?" she asked. "Modern consumerism I suppose."

Sometimes I forgot I was talking to someone from the 1600s. The concept of my world must seem foreign to her. But she seemed to understand that she was in a video game.

"Yeah, so we never actually spoke. But I know her nephew. It was kind of coincidental that I found out about her, but I've known him for almost a year."

105

"You really believe so? That it is coincidence?"

She smiled although her eyes still asked the question.

"I mean, well, shouldn't I? What do you mean? Does he know I'm a witch? Is that why he hung out with me today?"

"Oh, heavens, I've upset you. I'm sorry. I just meant that our kind generally believe there is no coincidence."

"So, that means he knows."

"Not necessarily. But I'm sure Fallon knows about your connection. And considering how much magic you're emitting right now, you may have drawn him to you."

"I thought...well, Julia said that I had to practice to give the magic a chance to escape. But I emit it, too?"

"She is correct. Practicing will give you a chance to use some of the energy trapped within. It should keep you from trancing when you don't choose to."

"Wait, I'll be able to choose to trance or not? Why would I want to do that?"

"I think we're getting ahead of ourselves a bit, but trancing focuses your power. Eventually you'll want to do it, but only when it is absolutely necessary."

I nodded. Oddly enough this was beginning to make some sense to me. If I needed extra power, I could trance and focus it all in one spot. But since it gathered constantly within me, I had to get rid of the excess so that I wasn't driven into a trance. Now, if I only knew what power or energy I actually had.

"So, do I have a specific power, or is it more like the force in *Star Wars*?"

"I am, unfortunately, not familiar with your allusion here. But I can say that most witches have a specific power. They represent one of the five points on the pentagram."

"I read about that. How the points represent all kinds of different things like the points on the body or the elements." I was happy to show I had some knowledge, but fascinated that she understood the concept of a video game, but no one had told her about Star Wars. I'd have to explain it to her one day.

"Yes, exactly. Generally, a witch will have the power of one element. But you, dear Elizabeth, are a witch from beyond the pentagram. You are different. You are special."

"Margaret, Margaret. Are you in there?" a loud male voice boomed from outside the cottage.

"Who's that?"

"Margaret. Let's not do this again. Let me in, Margaret. You know I'll find a way."

"Elizabeth, it's time for you to leave."

"Who is it, Margaret? Is he angry?"

"Elijah, you are not welcome here. Please go," she yelled toward the wooden door.

"You can't hide in there forever, Margaret. Let me in now!" He pounded loudly on the door which shook. It reminded me a bit of the three little pigs not allowing the wolf into their homes.

My anxiety grew as he pounded, and I felt myself getting dizzy again.

"Elizabeth," Margaret said, grabbing my hands in hers. "If there is magic within you, use it to help me now."

"How? I don't know how!"

"Focus. Shut your eyes and see him walk away within your mind. Use the force beyond the pentagram."

I was about to ask her what that meant. I was tired of reading and hearing it and having no idea what it meant.

Then the screen went black.

9

I LOOKED TO the door and found Ashley standing in the corner, the plug to the television in hand.

"Dammit, Ashley. What are you doing?"

I fumed and she just stood there with a dumb look on her face. To her credit, it was her normal look, but I found it especially dumb suddenly.

"I was trying to plug in my cell charger. I didn't realize it was the TV cord. I just thought it was the lamp. You're so touchy. What's your problem?"

"You," I said and turned off the console.

"Are you hanging around?" I asked my roommate coldly. I knew I sounded mean, but I just didn't have the patience it took to deal with her. It's like she sucked all of the energy out of me or something.

It was a loss to continue playing with Ashley there anyway. And I knew it was pointless to even think about practicing spells and incantations if she stayed in the room. I could look over the grimoire again, but she may get suspicious if she saw me reading a book without words. Margaret had said that I'd need my keeper to progress further anyway. I could get back to all of that later. Besides, I knew I should work on my statistics homework. I may be a witch, but I had no magical math powers as far as I could tell.

"Yeah, I'm totally exhausted. We partied pretty hard last night." She droned on about her night with the Zetas, eventually explaining their impromptu karaoke contest at Hancock's. That's when I broke in.

"I know all about your night at The Cock, Ashley. You puked on me, remember?"

"Oh, my God, gross. No way!"

"It was, and you did. You were on the sidewalk with your friends and you ran up to hug me. Then you puked."

"My bad," she said. "I guess I forgot that part. I don't remember much after leaving the bar."

I noticed how she didn't apologize.

"But you should have heard my version of 'Bad Romance'. I sounded just like Gaga. I swear."

Obviously we were ignoring the ride on the Vomitron and moving on.

"Great, Ashley. That's just great." Who wanted to sound like Gaga? I respect the woman for going about things her own way and all, but it has never been my kind of thing. That and you'd never catch me singing in public regardless of the song.

I tried to bury myself in my work, but Ashley's humming and singing kept me on edge. I noticed the annoyance building in me as I tried to block her out. I'd normally head out to see

Felix or Darcy at this point, but I knew both of my friends were busy with their own lives. Now I was annoyed and jealous. My grandmother had always said I was a moody girl, but I could feel these emotions mix inside me. The red annoyance and the green jealousy combined to an odd yellow light that I could feel surrounding me like an aura. It felt palatable and I wondered if Ashley could see it.

Ignorant to my shift in mood, she sang louder, ensuring I had a front row seat at today's Gaga cover show. Trying harder to ignore her, I sat down with my statistics book and did what I could. Somehow, the need to determine confidence intervals didn't have the same level of importance to me as it may have two days ago.

About an hour later, Ashley settled down, but by that point I couldn't focus on math anymore. The grimoire was calling to me. After fighting it this long, I decided to chance it. Ashley was engrossed in a reality TV marathon, watching rich women argue while on exotic vacations. She sat there, intensely focused on what the blonde one said the brunette said about the blonde with obviously fake boobs. Yet Felix didn't understand how I could dislike her. There were oh, so many, many reasons.

I grabbed the grimoire, trying to be nonchalant about the fact that I'd be reading a book written in writing only I could see that was left for me by a mystery witch I'd never met but whose nephew I had a major crush on. Nothing odd about that.

Placing it in my lap, I opened it to the middle. I tried to hide the fact that the pages were flipping themselves, opening itself to a page it felt was important for me to read. It landed on page 9, The Keeper.

"The keeper of the heir of Cassidy will show herself at her predestined time. She will not appear to all, but to the heir herself. The keeper of a witch beyond the pentagram must be called by Diana and will respond to the heir rather than the clan of keepers. She will know and understand the powers of her witch. She will protect and serve, although it may be in ways unlikely and unforeseen.

"The Witch of Clan Cassidy, the witch beyond the pentagram, will focus her energies safely while in proximity of her keeper. She will have the ability to bestow power to her keeper as well. This is unknown throughout our community as no other witch—no witch with a singular point of power—may do the same.

"The keeper of this witch will enjoy any powers awarded her until they are revoked. However, she will always contain the will and ability to read and speak the language of the forgotten scroll."

The forgotten scroll? Great, I had something else I had to figure out now. Like finding my keeper wasn't enough. At least

I knew more about her. And it sounded like we'd be different than most other witches and keepers. Made sense. I mean, what about any of this appeared normal? Why shouldn't my situation be even screwier than the typical witch and keeper relationship?

"Whatcha reading?" Ashley asked, walking over to me.

I tried to shut the book, but something wouldn't let me. I didn't dare struggle against it with her standing there. I'd look like a goon if I showed her that I couldn't close a book. It would be bad enough when she noticed that there weren't any words there.

The page did turn despite my attempts to restrain the grimoire from any self-directed actions.

"Uh, nothing. Just some notes." I figured she'd be least likely to care about math. She was, after all, a marketing major interested in fashion design, not statistics.

Distracted, Ashley ignored my response and went back to whatever she'd been doing. I looked out the window and found it had gotten far later than I'd known. I could see a beautiful full moon shining as it began to creep above the horizon. So, I had my full moon. Now, if Diana would just call my keeper, I'd be set.

A knock sounded at our door and Ashley rushed to open it. One of her Beta Zeta sisters stood there with a pizza box.

"Hey, girl. Come in," she told the tiny brunette. The pizza

box actually dwarfed her small frame.

"You up for some pizza, Ash?" she asked in a voice far larger than her size. My mind immediately went to the appropriateness of this pocket-sized person on the sideline of a football field being tossed through the air and leading cheers of "De-Fence, De-Fence."

"Always! I'm starved." Ashley opened the door wide and the small girl and huge box made their way into the room. "Want some, Lizzie?"

Shocked that she asked, I stammered a bit as I answered and tried to collect my books. "Oh, uh…well, no, nah. I'm going to hit the library. I really do need to get this stats work done. Thanks though. You guys enjoy."

"Okay. You're loss," the tiny person said, her voice filling the room.

I was halfway out the door when Ashley said, "Hey, wait. You forgot your notebook," and she grabbed the grimoire.

I reacted quickly, hoping to keep her from picking up the book. "No, I'm good. Got what I need."

She had it in hand already though and it snapped open with some force.

"What the hell?" She jumped with alarm.

I braced myself for the moment she noticed it was empty. I had spent more than an hour reading it right in front of her, and now she'd see nothing in it and really think I was a wacko.

But that isn't what happened.

She held the book open in both of her hands. She looked down for a moment, looked up at me with a+ curious expression, and said, "Hey, this isn't statistics."

The empty pages were going to get me in some trouble here.

Her expression grew curious and she asked, "Lizzie, what's a keeper?"

"A what?" I asked in shock. She could read the book. She must have seen the title on the page, page 9.

"A keeper. It says, 'The keeper of the heir of Cassidy…' "

I tore the book from her hand and ran down the hallway to the stairs. I wasn't giving her a chance to catch up with me at the elevator.

What did this mean? If Ashley could read the grimoire, she had to be magical. But what type of magic did she possess? Felix was magical, but he couldn't read it. Was she a demon? I could see that. She seemed to be sent from hell to directly interfere with my life. I didn't know if demons actually existed, but if so, I could be convinced that Ashley was one.

Maybe she was a witch too. But Fallon had said, on the first page, that the grimoire could only be read by the heir of Clan Cassidy. So, Ashley and I were related? That seemed too far-fetched to be true. Even I couldn't be in a modern version of *The Parent Trap,* where my twin and I were separated at birth and reunited as college roommates.

That left one option, and I hated it almost as much as the twin idea.

Ashley was my keeper.

That was the only option left. If she could read the grimoire, she had to be the heir or the keeper of the heir.

I made it the lobby and burst through the front doors. Outside the evening brought a chill claimed by New England autumns. The grass had been mowed earlier that weekend, and the scent of it still wafted through the campus. I ran down the cobblestone path toward the reflecting pond. I breathed deeply and sat on a stone bench in the quad. It seemed the perfect spot to try to figure out the rest of my bewitched life.

While I knew it would take far longer than the rest of the evening, I considered all that I now knew.

Felix, the best friend I'd ever have, was a shape shifting cat. Margaret had said he was my familiar.

Fallon, a mysterious witch with gamer ability akin to my own, had taken me for a mentee of sort and created a video game to explain my destiny. She was also the aunt of the boy of my dreams, the boy who had kissed me just today.

Margaret and her descendant, Julia, were both keepers, women who worked with and protected witches.

I had a keeper now as well. A keeper I loathed.

I had a keeper because I was a witch.

Eventually I'd have to get used to saying that. Thinking that. Knowing that.

I felt light headed and tried to push past the dizzy spell coming on. I opened the grimoire, remembering what Julia said about releasing my magic. Maybe if I read a little more I could stay upright.

I reread Fallon's first note.

"I, Fallon Airleas Sterling, do hereby entrust this grimoire to Clan Cassidy. May the wise mother bestow this book and all that is does contain upon the heir of Cassidy, she who shall be kept and the great force outside the pentagram."

As I read the last word, letters began to appear on the page below it. Shadows of inky script became clearer as I stared.

"Blessed be, Elizabeth Claire Scott. An' ye harm none, do what ye will."

The phrase sat in my mind until I read it aloud.

"An' ye harm none, do what ye will."

It felt natural, as though it were something I had already known.

It had been an eventful few days, and if they had taught me anything, I was sure my future would bring about even more excitement. Possibly more than I could handle.

I could blame it on chaos or life or fate. But it seemed pretty clear as I sat there alone, listening to the voices of people who didn't learn life-altering news, smelling the shift of the season, and feeling ultimately changed, that it hadn't been anything as mundane as that. The only thing to blame at this point was magic.

THANK YOU

I hope you enjoyed *Playing with Magic.*

If so, would you mind leaving a review? Readers love to hear what others think of a work, and word of mouth is an author's best friend!

Please look for Liza's story to continue in the second Midnight Witches tale, *Playing with Fire,* coming your way in 2016!

Thank you!

ABOUT THE WITCHING HOUR COLLECTION

Good witch. Bad witch. White magic. Black magic. Kitchen magic. Pick your potion. Ready for Halloween? The authors of the Blazing Indie Collective, who brought you the Falling in Deep Collection, are brewing up something new.

Check out all the novellas in The Witching Hour Collection coming October 2015:

Melanie Karsak: Witch Wood

Peggy Martinez: A Wee Bit of Magic

Claire C. Riley: Raven's Cove

Eli Constant: Sleeping in the Forest of Shadows

Margo Bond Collins: Witches' Kiss

Elizabeth Watasin: Charm School: The Wrecking Faerie

Erin Hayes: I'd Rather be a Witch

Carrie Wells: Playing with Magic

Evan Winters: The Witch of Bracken's Hollow

Minerva Lee: Spun Gold

Blaire Edens: The Witch of Roan Mountain

Poppy Lawless: The Cupcake Witch

ACKNOWLEDGMENTS

A huge thank you to my husband and children who not only put up with my imagination, but encourage me to use it. Thanks, Tony, Danny, Zac, and Nora.

Thanks also go to:
Melanie Karsak, my writing guru, Erin Hayes, a really cool writer girl, and all the other members of the "KCCC" including Gina Makowiec, Sally-Anne Cleveland, Martha Wells-Copeland, Angela Montale, Karyn Ott, and the Blazing Indie Collective.

My parents, sister and brother-in-law, and grandparents deserve some love!

Lastly, Jane *HLM-SF* Barksdale gets a big hug right here!

ENJOY A PEAK OF CHAPTER ONE

**AT THE HEART OF THE DEEP
BY CARRIE L. WELLS**

OUT NOW

ONE: ANYA

THE SMALL SHIP intrigued me. Hundreds of boats cross my path daily, but this one, trailing temperature gauges and current trackers, interested me more than others. Rather than merely floating, this boat had a purpose, a reason to be so close to my island. Of course, the blond man diving into the water definitely had something to do with my interest and maybe the boat's purpose, too. His long, lean body cracked the face of the water, and as he surfaced, his strong arms propelled him forward and away from the boat. Every afternoon he did the same thing, dive, swim, float, swim back. And every afternoon I watched as his fluid movements made almost no break in the ocean's surface while he cut long paths across it.

I had announced to the tribe that we had visitors close, and immediately the chatter began. Assuring them the boat's and crew's focus was research, or looked to be, I held off further inquisition with a promise to continue tracking their efforts.

I met the boat for five days and each day they came a little closer. Today they sat only twenty miles from Orotava. Close enough that Phoebe and Fiona decided to join me in my afternoon surveillance. The twins heckled me as I led them through the sea. We hung back far enough that their equipment couldn't track our presence.

"It's a long way to go for a man, Anya," Phoebe commented, laughing at me as we swam.

Her sister joined in. "Any distance is too far for a man."

Both knew I'd never had any interest in humans before. I was far more comfortable in the sea than walking on land, even on our own island full of mer. But this one, comfortable in the sea and almost questing to be a part of it, lured me. At the very least, he was lovely to watch and I could fantasize about adding him to my land life.

"Look, neither of you had to come with me. I'm just fine watching this sea god all on my own." I smirked back at my childhood friends, taunting them with my infatuation.

The three of us surfaced and watched him cut through the waves with capable, powerful movements. He looked at home with the water cradling his body.

"That's some human," Fiona commented, breaking into my daydream.

Phoebe seemed more awed than her appreciative twin. "He's, well, he's beautiful," she added. "Look how smoothly he moves. He's part fish."

"No, he's all human," I concluded. "If he were part fish, I could do more than stare."

"So true," Phoebe agreed. "Unless he was a Trisanthian. Your father would rather unite you with a human."

She had a point. Nishan, my father and the tribal council leader of the Obthaluse, wouldn't stand for his only daughter uniting with a rival mer, but he also wouldn't care much for a human son-in-law.

We continued to watch the boat and the swimmer until he turned and started back. We dove below the waves to be sure he didn't look up and find three gawking mermaids. I pushed the boundaries a lot, but we had never been caught by humans. Maybe today was the day to change that.

From below we saw his tanned legs stir the water and force him forward. His steady pace moved him quickly and we kept at a distance. That gave us a chance to move closer to the drifting boat in order to watch him climb aboard, my favorite part of the last few days. Granted, while my father made plans to attend the united tribal meetings, my research sessions on the island had lengthened, not leaving lots of time for fun.

The man reached the boat and lifted himself onto the diving platform. The sun on his wet hair turned it a golden, tawny yellow, almost the same color as my own.

Fiona let out her breath with a sigh. "Too bad he has legs. Nothing good comes with legs," she explained authoritatively.

Phoebe and I both chuckled a bit. He whipped his head in our direction and we quickly dipped below the surface. He squinted at the ripple we left in the water, but he turned away and continued to climb to the deck.

Someone called out to him as he toweled off. "Oh, hey, Luke. Glad you're back. Amir found something we want you to see."

"Luke," I repeated as I exhaled and watched him disappear into the boat's cabin.

"Luke, Luke, Luke," Phoebe chanted in a sing-song voice.

At least I had a name to go with the lovely face.

Fiona joined in. "Not a bad name. It suits him. Luke, the light-giver. Isn't that what it means?," she remarked thoughtfully.

"No idea, but I like it. It fits him," Phoebe added. Then she started singing, "Luke, the light-giver, looks lovely and luscious."

"Phoebe, seriously?" I asked, more than a bit annoyed by my normally sweet friend.

"Wow, Anya, you must really be smitten. You don't get ticked off that easily." She smiled, either at the thought of pushing my buttons or maybe because I was smitten. I'm not sure which, but she would derive pleasure from either scenario.

Pointing at the bow, suddenly, Phoebe added, "Look. The Sea Star."

Her sister responded, confused, "What? What about it?"

"It's the name of the boat. The Sea Star."

"Okay, and?"

"Well, and nothing really. But it's kind of cute that the boat is the Sea Star and Anya has that star mark. And did you see his tattoo? It was a sea star, too."

"Only you would find that cute, Phoebe," Fiona chided. She considered herself the practical twin, while Phoebe held the title of dreamer.

But Fiona was wrong. I noticed the boat's name the first time I followed Luke to it. My father called me Sea Star. He used the nickname more often when I was younger, but he resorted to it now and again. He gave me the name when I was born because of the small, star-shaped patch of dark scales on my tail. And now it linked me to Luke. It was such a little thing, but it tied us together in a small way.

"She's dreaming again, Phee."

Phoebe's voice called me back to reality and I watched the boat pick up speed. Fiona swam towards it, taunting us to join her. Not ready to back down, Phoebe and I joined, racing to see who could reach her first.

We came up on the boat quickly, far faster than any of us anticipated. Forgetting about the tracking equipment, we closed the distance, breaching the surface and playing in the waves like dolphin. I hoped that's what we looked like. That way, if anyone glanced behind the boat, they'd just assume they'd attracted curious dolphins rather than stalking mermaids.

Unexpectedly, Luke reappeared on deck. He looked at the sky, upset, and walked briskly to the stern, reading a tablet. By the time he looked up, Fiona and Phoebe were safe below the churning water. I, however, dove head first over the boat's wake, locking eyes with him in the process. Not the way to go unnoticed.

His deep brown eyes caught mine, holding them, holding me. I didn't look away when he leaned over the railing before climbing down to the dive deck. I knew he saw me. All of me. But in that moment, I wanted him to know. I wanted him to know everything.

www.ingramcontent.com/pod-product-compliance
Lightning Source LLC
Chambersburg PA
CBHW030537130626
46552CB00006B/2297